Also by Camille Mariani

Lucille's Lie
Aletha's Will
Pandora's Hope
Links To Death
Prelude To Murder
Invitation To Die

Astrid's Place

"We opened the door to a murder."

Camille Mariani

authorHOUSE®

AuthorHouse™
1663 Liberty Drive
Bloomington, IN 47403
www.authorhouse.com
Phone: 1-800-839-8640

First published by AuthorHouse   04/29/2011

ISBN: 978-1-4567-6561-3 (sc)
ISBN: 978-1-4567-6560-6 (hc)
ISBN: 978-1-4567-6559-0 (e)

Printed in the United States of America

Any people depicted in stock imagery provided by Thinkstock are models, and such images are being used for illustrative purposes only. Certain stock imagery © Thinkstock.

This book is printed on acid-free paper.

"We opened the door to a murder"

Dedicated to Al, with all my love.

No ear can hear nor tongue can tell the tortures of the inward hell!
Lord Byron

PROLOG

Jason had wondered if he would feel like a foreigner in the United States after thirty-seven years in South Korea, but nothing had changed. The future looked as promising here at home as it did that last day before going to boot camp.

When he married Mi Hi, they remained with her family. He had no skills and no plans for the future until he learned about a high-paying hit job and found that he was suited to the criminal life. Although his wife called him crazy for entering that first murder-for-hire contract, she enjoyed spending his high income from many similar jobs through the succeeding years.

Two months ago, however, after Jason contracted to end an old man's life, Mi Hi questioned his mental state once again. The shooting was quick and easy, but not the aftermath. Jason had made it a habit not to look into the eyes of his victims, but something was different this time. The dead man's stare was hypnotic, and Jason could not turn away. In horror, he watched the right eyeball roll out of its socket, float upward, and grow larger. He fled the scene, but the Eye followed him. Day and night it watched and haunted him. At last, unable to cope with it any longer, he asked his wife if she saw it, too.

Mi Hi said she did not see the Eye. But how could she *not* see it? Over and over again he pointed to it, hovering above them, always staring. With each denial, she tried Jason's patience to the breaking point. He grabbed her by the arms and ordered her to stop lying. The Eye was there. She *must* see it.

She screamed, "Stop this. You're acting crazy!"

He didn't plan to kill her, only to make her tell the truth, to admit that she could see what he saw. Why was she belittling him? He was in a frenzy to be vindicated. He knew he wasn't insane.

"Say you can see it," he demanded. "I'm not crazy. Tell me you see it."

His hands circled her neck. He repeated, "You *do* see it, you have to see it."

When she stopped struggling, he found that he was holding her dead weight. Looking back, he took solace in the knowledge that if her body ever should be netted from the sea where he dumped it, police would never net him. He was safe now at home in Fairchance.

ONE
TUESDAY, AUGUST 1, 1989

Watching Main Street activity, Astrid's excitement grew, and she thought, *This is the right place for me.* In all of Maine, she knew of no city like Fairchance. It captured her heart the day she interviewed for the newspaper reporting job. The daily scramble along Main Street reflected the city's vitality, while lamp posts with hanging baskets of red geraniums, and fresh colors on store fronts expressed pride and good taste. A neighborly country atmosphere prevailed in a city without big box stores and sprawling malls.

She studied the workers rushing to and from their individual destinations, as well as those less frantic strollers whose chief reason for frequenting the sidewalks was to stop friends and discuss the weather, politics, health issues--whatever topped the gripe list. Today, the wicked hot weather would be the topic, as if Maine had never bathed in ninety-degree humidity before, or that soon everyone would be in a state of self-pity over early signs of winter. However, Fairchance was no less alive than usual this afternoon. Sunlight bounced off auto windshields, like blinding camera flashes, while heat waves hovered above the softened pavement.

A chubby little boy in halter shorts slurped and savored

a melting chocolate ice cream cone. Shaded by her bent umbrella, a white-haired woman limped along among shoppers, unaware of the sidewalk traffic problem she caused. A leashed golden retriever panted alongside his master, and a shopkeeper unfurled the overhead canopy for shade.

Astrid barely noticed the temperature and humidity. Her thoughts centered on personal good fortune. For now, at least, she had a full-time job. If she could hold her tongue, she'd probably keep the job another week or so. But that was just the problem. To remain silent when she felt the urge to blurt out what she thought would restrict her sense of rightness. Much easier to let loose, expose herself to ridicule, even possible dismissal, than to act demure and remain passive in a clearly objectionable situation.

Her rough manner and blunt talk often resulted in alienation of others, even employers, leaving her with little confidence that she could compete in anything but sports, or work at much of anything but farm labor. However, this was different. Here in Fairchance, she was determined to break the pattern, to try harder, and to conquer this blemish on her character, her social life, and her work environment. At the age of twenty-eight, she should be able to REFORM. Damn. That might be too much. But that's exactly what she must do. She reminded herself daily to button it and not offend.

Despite her self-doubt, she was about to make the leap from living at her brother's farm to owning her own home. It wouldn't be a very costly place, no more than a structure that she could fix up and call her own. It had long been her goal to own property of her own. Perhaps now she could achieve that dream. It didn't take long to recognize that Fairchance offered a good life, an ideal location to plant roots. Not only were people friendly here, but it was a community offering amenities generally found only in larger cities. Main Street brought neighbors together. Children played unsupervised.

Waiting for an agent at the Fair Hills Realty Office, Astrid stood at the front window and observed that high temperatures motivated women to wear shorts and halters, gauzy dresses and strap sandals, and to show off varying shades of red skin from sunbathing. All of which she avoided. Skimpy summer clothing would look ridiculous on an already ridiculous feminine frame, as she saw it, and her fair skin burned far too easily and too painfully to be tolerated.

"Hello, my name is Holly Rutherford. I'll be happy to help you today."

The soft voice behind her sounded way too friendly.

Astrid turned and saw a perfect size eight, in perfectly wrinkle-free light blue summer suit. The sight prompted her to smooth the wrinkles from her loose, button-up cotton top.

"Hi there, Holly."

She grabbed the young woman's hand. It reminded her of a rubber doll's empty skin.

"I'm Astrid Thorpe. Just started as a reporter at *The Bugle*, and I want to buy a house. I thought, hell, why not?

Fairchance is going to be my hometown now, so why not just plunge in and become a homeowner. Ya?"

Holly's face registered surprise. She took a step backward, while her widening eyes looked Astrid up and down.

"I see. Well."

Astrid feared she had been too loud, too coarse, too much for the little woman, who looked wobbly on very high heels. It would be no particular surprise if Holly ran out the back door.

"Follow me to my office and we'll go over some properties together. Tell me what you're looking for."

"Sure, but I can tell you right now, don't haul out those high-priced mini-mansion brochures. I want a fixer-upper. Something real cheap, to be honest. If it has a roof to keep the rain out, that's about all I want. I'm not poor, understand, just not extravagant."

If the little lady sighed because she thought Astrid hardly worth bothering with, she would have been overwhelmed to learn that this farmer's daughter had inherited a fortune from her grandfather, a man who never shied from hard work. When he and his bride came from Sweden, he bought a farm in the Appleton area. In time, he reinvested money in more land, and hired more farm workers so that he could diversify and create an agricultural products brand name. In his lifetime, he amassed his fortune through work and frugality. He loved his granddaughter, and she trusted him with her innermost secrets. Once, when she was twelve, she went to him and cried because she was so much bigger than any of her classmates. Some kids, she told him, were calling her "Big ass Astrid."

Grampa Thorpe, whose frame had already deteriorated, pulling him downward in a gradual slide from life to death, said in his sing-song Swedish rhythm, "Don't pay attention to them. In a few more years you will be beautiful. Ya, you will be yust like your lovely grandmother. Stand tall and proud always, and be as strong as you are tall."

Of course, it was a good fix at the time, and Astrid began to walk with a longer stride, to hold herself straighter, and to bellow when she talked. It did intimidate some of the bullies, and those who weren't impressed found that her fist could deliver a painful nosebleed. She understood now that what Grampa told her was nothing but a carrot of hope for her conflicted emotions.

In college, she was the tallest, fastest, highest scoring player on the women's basketball team. Basically, she was loved by fans and hated by most teammates for stealing all the attention and awards. Today, she had no illusions about her looks or much of anything beyond her own integrity. She turned down a chance to join a pro team because she wanted to write, not play basketball. She knew that other pro players would be better than she was, and eventually she would have to give it up. Writing had a lasting future that basketball couldn't equal. However, income wasn't one of the perks of this chosen field.

"Well now," Holly said with a less happy lift to her voice, "there isn't a lot for sale among low-priced homes. I can show you three. Do you want to see them today?"

"Ya. I sure as hell do."

The first one was barely standing, three miles out in the country, so Astrid explained that she preferred a place closer to town. She could live at the edge of the city, but not this far out, and even though she had said she wanted a fixer-upper, she didn't really want a tar papered shack.

On outer Main Street, south past a garage and a lumber company, Holly unlocked the door to a gray two-story house, not in bad condition, but definitely without character. Astrid dutifully looked all around, nodding in each plain box-like room, as if somewhat interested. Then she said she'd prefer "something a bit different, thank you."

On Lilac Lane, one of the city's several cul-de-sacs, they came to the third house, and as they approached it, Astrid sat up straight, hitting her head on the ceiling of the new compact car. This was a once-beautiful home with an upstairs three-window gable over a similar three-window bay on the ground floor, fireplace on the left side, and on the right, a recessed entry to the front door with a lead glass window.

Holly slowed the car and narrated like a tour guide.

"Francis Guilford, the man who built the houses on this street, owned all this land and actually created the street. He planted a lilac bush in front of each house and that led to the naming of the street. What happened was, after inheriting the land from his mother, Guilford began to order Sears Roebuck house kits…you know, prefab houses. He would build one and sell it at a profit, then another, make more money, and so-on, until he had made and sold six, three on each side of the street. Then he bought a more impressive house package and built this one for himself. As you see, the other houses are more like cottages. He brought his bride here, but after a few years, he left her quite suddenly. She lived here until she went into a nursing home. I believe she's in Bangor."

"You mean you could look through the Sears catalog, find a house plan you liked, and actually order it, then wait for UPS to deliver it in boxes full of wood?"

"Well, I'm not sure if there was UPS then, but yes, that's how it worked. I think the kit would likely have come via rail."

"Oh ya, of course. I remember trains. They were those more efficient, faster systems that the auto industry killed so that we can battle traffic for hours in our big cars and pollute the environment, and feel a helluva lot safer and happier driving around big tractor trailer rigs."

Holly laughed, but nodded and said, "Right on."

Astrid was pleased to see Holly warming to her.

"What happened to Mr. Guilford? Why did he leave his wife and this lovely home? Sounds like a damned fool, if you ask me."

"No one but Mrs. Guilford knows the answer to that. She told everyone that he had gone to Alaska and intended to return when he had made a fortune. Many people thought that was strange since he was one of the city's richest men. Anyway, he never did return, and everyone assumes he died there in Alaska. She never remarried."

"Looks like Mrs. Guilford didn't get much of his money. A lot of repair needs to be done to this one. Still, I like the lines. It must have been very pretty years ago."

"Yes, I think it was. She lived here many years, and the house has been empty for nine years. That hasn't done it any good. They tell me she worked, but not at a very high-paying job. Maybe he sent her money. I don't know. To say the least, she left the property in bad condition. She wouldn't sell until just recently because she thought she might be able to come back some day. Of course, she never did and never can now. I heard that she isn't expected to live much longer, and I think most likely the money from the sale of the house will go to the nursing home."

Astrid opened the door on her side.

"As you see by the listing sheet, there are two acres of land here," Holly said. "It goes beyond that big pine tree on the east to Elm Street and extends north across the empty lot to Spring Street where you see the two-and-a-half-story house. And the empty lot goes west to the fire station. There's a stone wall along most of the boundary lines. Mr. Guilford had planned to expand his housing development along the Spring Street side, but he never did. There's not too much property left with this much land in the city now."

"It's perfect," Astrid said as soon as she got out of the car. "This will do."

"You may change your mind when you see the inside. We list it 'as is.' Nothing was done to fix it up or clean it out because Mrs. Guilford stipulated that we not take anything out of the house before selling it. She even said to leave papers in the desk. There's not much furniture left, since she sold most of it before going into the nursing home. She's a strange one."

"Doesn't matter. I know this is it. This is the place I'll call home."

TWO
WEDNESDAY, AUGUST 23, 1989

This was the right address. A wood slab, protruding from a freshly planted row of pansies, bore the single name Thorpe. Someone had hacked away at the lawn and started a flower garden. But this place needed a major overhaul. Some of it looked as if it didn't need a carpenter so much as a demolition crew. The lady had said over the phone, "I need a few house repairs."

Abram scratched his head, and contemplated whether he really wanted to bother with this Astrid Thorpe at all. Looked like it would be a lot of work, judging from sections of crumbling cellar wall, missing roof shingles, and zig-zagging chimney top. White paint was a distant memory. This was just outside. The interior must be a beaut.

On the other hand, he had only one job lined up for next week and nothing beyond that. It was galling to think that everyone must be a do-it-yourselfer these days. Practically all the money he had jingled in his pocket. He needed employment, and with any luck this woman could pay him regularly, unlike his last job.

"Well," Abram intoned. "Obviously, the poor lady needs help. So let's get to it."

He slid out of the truck and went to the front door.

When it opened to his knock, he nearly forgot how to talk. In front of him stood a tall, lean blond, in red plaid camp shirt and jeans. He was taller than most men at six-three, and here he was, looking into her midnight blue eyes. She brushed aside silky strands of hair flying from a braid that circled her head several times. He'd like to see all that hair loose. With her full bosom and flushed milk-white skin, her quick smile that flashed perfectly aligned teeth, she could not ever be mistaken for a mannish Amazon.

But when she spoke, Abram thought he could have sized her up wrong.

"You must be Lincoln, ya?" It sounded like she was shouting the words to someone down the street. "Come in. I've been at it since sunrise. Had to drive here from South Appleton. Sick and tired of this commuting business. But I'll be damned if I go back tonight. I've been cleaning the back bedroom upstairs where I'll sleep, if the new bed ever gets here today. Well, this is no palace, but it's all mine."

She swept her hand around for him to take a look.

"You'd think a body could have something more impressive to be proud of, huh? I'm like my grampa, though. I'll make the most of it with a bit of hard work. Can't keep a Swede down by a simple case of hard work ahead."

For some reason he never would understand, the name Rapunzel popped into Abram's mind. It had been many years since his mother read that story to him. Standing just inside the doorway, he shifted his eyes from Astrid's crowning glory to piles of wallpaper and ceiling plaster in the middle of the living room floor. Beyond the French doors, he could see a bit of the dining room, in similar condition. The carpet smelled like wet dog. He glanced down at the faded, grimy vestibule carpet.

"Should I take off my shoes?" he asked.

It was a pleasure to see her laugh like that, pure brightness.

After his quick assessment of problems from the foyer, Abram said, "A bit of hard work? Looks more like twenty-four/seven of intensive hard labor to me. You really plan to renovate this place?"

The light went out of her eyes as she took a mental inventory of what he saw. Made him want to put his arm around her and say he didn't really mean it was beyond fixing. But just as suddenly as she fell glum, the sparkle returned, and, if possible, the words thundered more.

"Ha. I see you're plain talking, just like me," she said. "Ya. I plan to renovate this place, all right. You think you're up to it? If you don't think so, I'll find someone else."

Abram studied her again. The voice was a hog caller's, but the body and face should be on a runway, modeling some outlandish creation, and striking a pose that showed off those long legs. Not an ounce of fat on her, everything solid, including her hand grip that had nearly taken him to his knees.

"Did you have it inspected before you bought it?"

"Hell, no. I knew it would fall over in a good wind. But I figure this way. For what I paid, it's worth whatever it takes to bring it back. The land alone is worth the price.

If you're willing to take it on, I want a new foundation poured out back. I want to move the house back from the street and get rid of this dirt cellar, if it's structurally sound, that is. I want a circular driveway, you see. And I want a new garage. That chimney will come down, and I want a large rock fireplace at the side of the living room, where that one is. You know a mason, do you?"

Abram nodded. This project was taking on proportions he hadn't expected. Just processing the sequence of each proposed change had him mentally putting on the brakes. What was the woman thinking? Alone and needing all of this done? Could she really afford it? Why not buy a cottage, all upgraded?

"I have a good mason who works with me some."

"I'll have central heat with an oil furnace in the basement and auxiliary heat from the fireplace. Always loved a fireplace. We had a big one on the farm. Spent a good many evenings in front of it doing my homework. Well, come on. Let's take a look around before you say yea or nay. It's no damn good just standing here and looking at it. You'll need to do some pulling down, you know."

He knew. Right away, he saw that the powder room to the right of the foyer had the original wood-seat toilet with tank overhead and a chain attached. Going from room to room downstairs and up, he envisioned spending the rest of the year right here, maybe the better part of next year, for that matter, 'pulling down.' But it had a certain appeal now. In all that time, he'd be working with this gold-framed loudspeaker. It wouldn't all be hard work. He'd make sure of that.

"You work days, do you?" he asked.

"Ya. At *The Bugle*. I'm a reporter. Haven't been there long, but it's great. I think each day, after I get home, we'll discuss what you'll do the following day. If you can stay beyond five o'clock, I'll work with you for an hour before you leave. You know, some things need two pairs of hands instead of one. I'm a good worker. Been doing it all my life on the farm."

"Sounds fair enough to me. But I do have a helper who will be here some with me."

"Sure. I see. Now I guess we should discuss what you expect to get for all this work," she said. Her eyes warned, *Don't fleece me or I'll kill you.*

Abram laughed at the thought, fully appreciating her unspoken meaning.

"Don't get me wrong, Miss Thorpe."

He looked down at the floor while he mulled it over.

"I just thought it odd that the last thing you brought up was payment. Most people ask about the cost before they let me inside. This is going to take a long time, and I hate to charge by the hour at my usual rate, considering that you're a working woman. Tell you what. I don't need a lot to live on, just between you and me, so why don't you pay me a weekly rate. Say, four hundred a week for labor, plus the cost of supplies. It's about half what my hourly rate would come to. And when I need my helper, it's an added ten dollars an hour."

She tilted her head in a coquettish manner, though he was certain she had no thought of flirting.

"You must be kidding," she said. "Or do you plan to work a four-hour day?"

He laughed again.

"No way. I'll give you a good day's work, believe me. I might ask for one more thing, though, at that price."

"What?"

"How about throwing in supper each night after six?"

Now it was her turn to laugh. Her candid manner and bright smile could brighten a man's life, and he could use some cheer in his.

"Ya. You bet. I'll make you a good supper."

Abram walked out to the steps, and she followed.

"By-the-way, what do they call you? Abe?"

"They call me Abram," he said. "Do they call you A...?"

"No." She quickly cut off the word. "They call me Astrid. So we're on a full first-name basis, then."

He got into his truck, and, wearing a broad grin, backed out of the short driveway.

* * *

Astrid tried to sleep, but this first night in her new home was hot. It not only felt strange, but somehow threatening. No, that wasn't the right word. Not so much threatening as magnetic, pulling at her. What a silly notion, she thought, staring up at the exposed ceiling slats where plaster had fallen away. With her arms behind her head on the pillow, she tried to determine what it was that niggled at her now, something she hadn't noticed before.

She was never afraid of new surroundings, nor anxious over change. But something about this house felt wrong. It wasn't just the occasional thump and scrambling in the walls that disturbed her. Some people claimed to have ESP, but the subject held no interest for her, nor did she believe in it for a minute. Yet, if she were to define her present anxiety, she would have to admit that the foreboding was of something having gone terribly wrong here in the past, or of something that soon would go wrong. Or both.

"The house can't be haunted. There's no such thing as a haunted house," Astrid said with a roaring laugh.

The heavy and musty air wrapped around her like a wool sweater, even with the windows open. Maybe because the house had been empty for several years, she imagined some mysterious presence. Then she laughed again.

"Ya. Mice, no doubt. Well, little guys, either clear out now or face the trap tomorrow."

Despite her bluster, she was nervous, and she couldn't laugh about that. So she told herself to think about something else. Think about Abram Lincoln. She recalled that when he went down to the cellar and returned he said she was right. She needed either to have this rock foundation re-laid, or build a new one, but everything about the structure of the house itself was sound. An electrician would be needed to see if the wiring would pass inspection. Then, of course, the plumbing should be inspected, and they already knew the fixtures were old. When the house was built, everything was top-of-the-line. Now, everything was dated thirties: black kitchen woodstove, a small gas stove, black sink with single faucet for cold water, claw-foot bathtub and no shower, linoleum with worn-black holes in the kitchen, and creaky pine floors in upstairs bedrooms.

If she were a crying woman, she'd do it now. The enormity of work facing her seemed too much, despite her earlier boast to Abram. She had big ideas, but would it all be doable? And what was she trying to do, after all? She'd probably be penniless when it was all finished.

Then there was the troublesome thought that she could lose her job any time. After all, there was no contract that said she'd have it for even a full year. There was no guarantee that she'd live up to Natalie's expectations. Her boss was a very efficient editor. Astrid had learned that already. But would they be compatible in the long run?

"Stop this damned foolishness!"

She told herself to remember that she'd been up and going since five this morning, and it was now past midnight. Being overly tired made one weak and vulnerable, so that even small problems loomed as insurmountable. It would all look better in the light of a new day.

She mustn't forget to nail a temporary replacement step over that broken one in the stairway. Abram said he'd fix it, but then forgot to do it before he left.

She sighed the words, "It could be worse."

Or could it? Had she been a damned fool taking on a broken-down old house? At the moment it felt like she was facing a mountain that she had to tunnel through with a nail file.

Abram's image came to mind, and she closed her eyes. Tall, muscular, and well tanned from working outdoors, he was a helluva handsome man, even in green work clothes. She always admired seal brown eyes, and his squinted almost shut when he laughed. She found him to be unsettling, with a sense of humor that left her wondering whether he was serious or joking. The best part of it all was that she would see him every day, they'd have supper together, and they'd talk about the renovations. Damn. It sounded almost like man and wife stuff. As a bride, she might get away with being among the world's worst cooks, but with Abram she wasn't so sure. Anyway, she'd give it a try and if he lasted for supper more than one day, then maybe he had a stronger constitution than any man she'd entertained before. She thought, *It won't be all bad.*

THREE
THURSDAY, AUGUST 24, 1989

She arrived at the office five minutes early, tired, aching in places that never ached before, and not feeling fresh like she would if she'd had a shower. Even though she had to wait for a new gas stove and refrigerator, the store did send over the bed, but it wasn't as soft as she thought it would be, and she wondered if they had made a mistake and sent over the wrong one instead of what she tested earlier in the week. Nevertheless, Astrid put on a smile and spoke as softly as she could manage.

"Good morning, Natalie. A little hot, but a good one just the same."

It wasn't easy taking on this new persona. Who spoke in a whisper all the time, anyway?

"Morning, Astrid. I've never seen a summer like this in Maine. So changeable. We're having a new window air conditioner installed today. That should make it tolerable, at least."

"Ya. That'll help for damn sure. Oh." She slapped a hand over her mouth.

"I mean, for sure."

Natalie looked away, but Astrid saw the grin.

"So how do you like your new home?" Natalie asked. "You slept there last night?"

"I'll get used to it, I'm sure. Just a bit strange at first. The carpenter came by and we laid out some of the work that needs to be done. It will be a long while before I have a house-warming, I guarantee."

She went on, vaguely aware that her decibel level was rising with each sentence.

"Did you know you could order a house through the Sears catalog years ago? I never knew it. But that's what I have, a mail order house from Sears Roebuck. The guy that put it together did a good job, according to Abram Lincoln. He's the carpenter the hardware storekeeper recommended. Said it's sound, but the masonry isn't as good as the rest of the house. Anyway, by the time we're finished with it, it will all look new again. I'm bent on that, for damn sure."

She realized what she said, but this time she let it pass since Dee had come in, all smiles.

"Morning, Dee," Natalie said. "Astrid has just been telling about her new house."

"Ya. Hi, Dee. I forgot to tell anyone that it's a Sears mail order house. You could order them through the catalog in the old days."

Dee nodded.

"Yes, I know someone who has a Sears house. It's very nice. So that's what you have, Astrid."

"Ya. We'll get it in shape after a fashion. I'll be helping when I go home after five each day. And I never heard of giving the carpenter supper, but that's what he wants in place of a lot of money. Not a bad deal, I say. Besides…"

No, she shouldn't say that. Shouldn't speak of Abram's

being a handsome guy. They might get the wrong impression.

"Besides what?" Dee asked.

"Oh, besides, I like to cook for more than one."

Whew. Where'd that come from? She disliked cooking, but guessed she could do as well as the next woman if she really put her mind to it. Her poor mother had been so disappointed with the lack of interest Astrid showed in food preparation.

"Well," Natalie said, "things are quiet around here now. In fact, you don't really need to come in on Thursdays, unless there's a breaking story to cover."

"But…"

Astrid stopped short of saying that she would need all the money she could get now. It wasn't strictly true, but she had budgeted with her income in mind. There was no need to let everyone in on her financial status. However, Natalie understood. She always seemed to have a sixth sense about things.

"Don't worry about your salary. As often as you get Thursday off, you'll likely have to work overtime or on a weekend. It all balances out, and we leave it at that. Take time off when you can get it. Now, Astrid, I have a couple of assignments for you, both for next week's issue. Here's a request for a photographer to cover a ribbon cutting for the opening of a new flower shop. They're calling it simply Flowers. Not very imaginative, huh?"

Dee had settled at her desk by the window, and was typing some notes on the computer.

"Unimaginative," she said. "But that says it all, doesn't it? Almost like Tim Sample's generic *Book*."

Astrid winked in an exchange of glances with Dee. Apparently Dee, like herself, was a fan of the Maine humorist.

Natalie continued without comment on the book.

"We always run the fall schedule for high school basketball. This is a good chance for you to meet the coach, Will Stockton. You can do that right after the flower shop opening. The games should be scheduled by now. It's almost time for school to start up again. Can you believe it? Seems like the summer just started, and now we're thinking of fall schedules. Don't be put off by Stockton, Astrid. He comes on strong and can be intimidating."

Astrid said simply, "Ya?"

Natalie and Dee laughed in unison. Astrid looked up, but could see no offense in their attitude, so they must be laughing at the thought of anyone's intimidating her.

* * *

Friday, August 25, 1989

Gardening and flowers were among Astrid's interests, and the flower shop interview had been a pleasant experience. She was still thinking about all the arrangements Alice Fawn made, and how pretty it looked and how sweet it smelled as she parked her Jeep behind the Fairchance High School gym. Alice said her dream had long been to open such a shop, but with the heavy cost of setting up, now she was worried that her business acumen might not be strong enough. Astrid assured her that she couldn't miss, since it was the only commercial hot house for twenty-five miles, and, because of its location across the street from the hospital, her cut flowers should sell well to hospital visitors.

Walking to the gymnasium side door, Astrid felt a pang of insincerity. She surely hoped she was right in what she said to Alice. Apparently the woman didn't have a great deal of capital going into the operation, and everyone knew that without capital to cover five years of operation, a business could easily fold before it had time to become profitable. However, the floral business should flourish in a community like this, where colorful flowers decorated everything from Main Street lamp posts to window boxes. You could never really be certain about such things.

Stopping at the door, she took a look around. This was so familiar, the long gym attached to the two-story brick school, a yellow school bus parked and ready for passengers, probably going to a summer sports seminar. The tennis courts behind the gym surprised her, though. Not many high schools had those. She took a deep breath when she looked up at the gym's screen-covered windows. She didn't need this nostalgia, nor did she like the feeling of having sacrificed acclaim and high income for a job that many, including her brother, saw as inferior to sports stardom. Well, money be-damned, she made the right choice, her own choice. A writer she would be, and that was that. At least she didn't have to worry that a serious injury could mean the end of working in her field. She squared her shoulders, said, "Damn," several times, and opened the door.

A barrel-chested man was just entering the gym from a door at the side, and Astrid called to him.

"Sir. Can you tell me where I might find Coach Stockton?"

He turned his angry face toward her. Through clenched teeth, he said, "In there," and nodded toward the door he had closed behind himself.

"Thanks."

What a sullen man, Astrid thought. As she walked across the gym floor, she saw the sign, Coach, above the door. It couldn't be plainer.

To her knock, a voice yelled, "It's open."

A man sat pulling folders from a dented gray file cabinet, his back to the door. The way he flung each file to the floor clued Astrid that he might be upset, just like the other man.

"Well?" he said.

"I take it you're Coach Stockton?"

"So? You want something? Make it quick."

He rolled his chair back to the desk and looked up at her. He was no young man, probably had tenure, Astrid thought. His butch cut showed more gray than black over a deeply tracked forehead.

"I'm Astrid Thorpe. I'll be covering sports for *The Bugle* this year, and I came over to pick up your fall basketball schedule."

He looked at her with contempt, as if she had asked him to give her the keys to Fort Knox.

FOUR

Abram sat on the bank of Rapid River to eat his two bologna sandwiches and drink a thermos of milk for lunch. Work at the hardware store had progressed faster than he figured it would, thanks to Joe Plunket, a sales clerk, who'd saved him time by removing everything from the side of the room where he wanted built-in cases. At this rate, Abram decided, he could start work on Astrid Thorpe's house about the middle of next week. The renovation would ordinarily be tedious but not overwhelming. However, with the shoulder pain he'd been experiencing for the past two weeks, it might be more difficult than it should be.

When Abram had spoken of having difficulty raising his arm due to the shoulder pain, his barber commented, "Y'know, I had the same thing. Went to the doctor and ended up in physical therapy for two months. Somehow I'd torn the cuff. Let's see, what th' devil did he call it? Ahh, rotation cuff."

He stood back and looked at Abram in the mirror, while holding up the shears much like a surgeon holding a scalpel.

"Ayuh. That's it. Rotation cuff. About the worst pain I ever had. You've prob'ly got the same thing."

Two months of physical therapy would be more than he could afford. In fact, he couldn't afford to be out of work for more than a week, which was why the job for Astrid Thorpe was so important to him.

Astrid Thorpe. Independent women didn't appeal to Abram as a rule. What he'd seen were bossy, sure to tell you that they knew a lot, and of no sex appeal to him. Some men found them desirable, but he couldn't abide a woman…or a man, for that matter…who was self-important, talking down to others,

But this Astrid. Now, she personified the fist in a silk glove. Smooth, glowing, the genuine article. And when she opened her mouth, you'd better stand back a foot or two. Good lord, if he was around her long, he might go deaf. That wasn't such a wonderful thought. Yet, if something had to go, it could be worse than hearing. At least then he could enjoy her in all other ways and not hear a word she said.

"Wonder why she does talk so loud," he said, as he mused about this woman who occupied his thoughts most of his non-working hours, and even some of those, too. "Doesn't she hear herself?"

He screwed the cup cover onto the thermos bottle and put it, along with his empty sandwich bags, into his lunch bucket. Lunch over, he had a few minutes to relax before going back to the store. He liked the creativity of carpentry. And, being self-employed, it gave him freedom to do other things between jobs. The trouble was that lately there had been more between jobs than working times. If it hadn't been for Astrid, he would be facing one of those periods, but now he'd be occupied for several months, and have the pleasure of a couple of hours a day with an interesting woman, to say nothing of a hot meal. How much better could it get?

Sitting cross-legged under a shady oak tree, he watched the rushing water swirl over smooth, shiny rocks. Like a kid, he plucked a blade of green grass from time to time, tossed it into the pure water, following its twists and turns until it slowed and floated in a calm pool. He felt the total peace of gurgling brook, warm sunshine, and singing birds. It would be nice to stay here all afternoon, and just be one with nature again, like old times. Some day he'd bring a fishing pole with him, like he used to, and catch speckled trout again. That was before his brother became ill.

It was soon time to go back to work. This job for Jake's Hardware had just one problem. While the wall shelves were going well and quickly, the next phase wouldn't be so easy. Jake wanted Abram to tear out part of the wall so that the front store would expand into the storage room. Maybe he'd miscalculated the time it would take him to do it. He wanted to begin work for Astrid a week from now. In his mind's eye he could see Jake's archway and knew how to build it, but now that he thought of the details, it might take two or three more days than he planned.

He arrived at the store just as the town clock struck one. Right on time. He picked up his hammer and began pounding nails into the one shelf yet unfinished. Shards of pain shot through his shoulder and arm.

"Damn. What's going on?"

This just couldn't happen to him. He had to work.

Without income he would have no apartment, no food, no anything. Poor Woody. It wasn't his fault that he came down with cancer. But his brother's long illness left Abram without savings. He was still paying the hospital what he could each month, and that was just the hospital bill.

So he couldn't slow down for a little pain. After work, he'd go to the pharmacy and get some aspirin…anything that would keep him going. For now, grin and bear it.

"Hey, down there."

Abram looked up. Jake's son Mickey peered at him over the edge of the storage loft where lumber and seldom-needed hardware items were kept.

"What's up, Mickey?"

"I need a hand. Got a box to get down there. I'll drop it down to you. Okay?"

Abram didn't see him go up to the loft. Must have done that when he was out. He should ask how heavy the box was, but the teenage boy had a habit of ridiculing others. He'd have a field day telling how weak Abram was if he even asked the question.

"Just a minute. I'll come over there."

He went to that end of the room and positioned himself with legs wide apart in order to steady himself.

"Okay. You can drop it now."

Mickey shoved it over the edge, and Abram caught what had to be at least a fifty-pound weight. He fell forward and let go of the box, he himself crashing over it like a dead tree limb in a hurricane.

"God, oh God," he screamed in pain. "What's in the box?"

Mickey was laughing as he lowered a ladder and climbed down.

"Thought you was a tough guy, Abram," the boy said, still laughing. "Guess a box of tiles was too much for ya."

Barely able to speak, Abram said, "Get your dad, Mickey. I need help."

"I was only kidding around. What happened? What's the matter?"

"Just get your dad, for God's sake. Now."

Abram's shoulder felt like it had been pulled out of his body. His arm dangled, lifeless, useless at his side. The excruciating pain was almost too much to bear. He tried to get up, but the room began to whirl. All he could do was lie there and wait for help. And all he could think was *How can I work now?*

FIVE

In the hallway, Astrid heard a heavy discussion coming from the editorial room, but she couldn't distinguish the words. She hesitated about entering in case it was very private. But, after all, she did work here and if they wanted privacy, they should have gone to the other room.

"Oh," she said, when she found a man talking with Natalie and Dee. "Am I interrupting?"

"Not at all," the man said. "Come in. Astrid, isn't it?"

He stood up and held out his hand.

"I'm Marvin Cornell, the…"

"Publisher," Astrid said hastily. "Glad to meet you, Mr. Cornell."

Moments like this, meeting someone of importance, felt awkward to Astrid, and she wasn't sure what to say.

"Damned hot weather," she sai.

Oh, no. That was wrong. She flicked a glance at Natalie and was relieved to see that she didn't have a disgusted look on her face.

Cornell nodded.

"Hot, but as they say, just wait fifteen minutes. It will change."

With that he laughed, and turned to Dee.

Dee left her desk and walked to him to shake his extended hand.

"Well, Dee, if you've finally made up your mind, then I won't try to dissuade you any longer. I wish you well. And success with your book."

"Thank you, Marvin. I appreciate that."

He left without further discussion, and Astrid stood where she was, looking at the door after he closed it. So that was the publisher. Nice man, smooth as silk in natty suit and tie. A bit on the short side, but nice all the same.

"How did it go with Coach Stockton?" Natalie asked. "Did he give you a hard time?"

"Tried to, but after all was said and done, he told me the fall schedule isn't complete yet. I can pick it up next week."

"Tell me about it. Was he polite? What did he say to you?"

Why was Natalie being so inquisitive about this? Astrid worried that he had already called her and complained.

"I wouldn't say that exactly. He said *The Bugle* was a rag, and he doesn't subscribe to it any more. And at first he just said no, he wouldn't give me the schedule."

"And what did you say?" Dee asked.

Now Astrid was really worried. Pressing the issue like this could mean only one thing. She was in trouble. Well, might as well face up to it.

"I told him he was a weasel as far as I was concerned. And I said I knew how politics works in education, and that his superiors do read our rag, as he called it. I also said I would be happy to editorialize about how the high school basketball coach had the manners of a two-year-old. Anyway, when I finished, I said we should start over, and he should tell me why he wouldn't give me the schedule. I added that he should do it sweetly."

The two women, listening with growing delight, burst into laughter.

"I told you," Dee said. "I knew she could do it."

"You mean I'm not in trouble?" Astrid said.

"Not at all. That man never says a pleasant word to anyone. He needed dressing down. We've locked horns before, and he has the attitude that he can do no wrong. I'm glad you explained that he would do wrong if he crossed you. Good job. You'll have to excuse us, but we had a bit of a discussion on whether you'd put him in his place."

Natalie wiped a tear from her eye.

"Did you think he had complained, Astrid?"

"Ya. I did. You know I do come on a bit too strong myself sometimes."

Another round of laughter, and Natalie said, "You needn't have worried. That man would be mortified to complain that a woman came into his office and left him ready to throw up his hands. It just wouldn't be manly."

"Ya. I understand."

Each day here at *The Bugle* brought a whole new outlook for Astrid. It was the first time that she had genuine support since her grandfather died, and it felt good. The family had been held together by Grampa, though his own son was disrespectful and critical of how he ran things, and Astrid's brother Gunnar had little interest in the land after he inherited all of it. After Grampa died and left Astrid quite comfortable with her inheritance, the farm was neglected by her brother Gunnar, to Astrid's dismay. She had worked alongside the men as she grew up and would have been as happy with the farm as with the money, but when she was left to pursue other avenues, she went on to college.

All the while they talked about Astrid's meeting with the coach, she was wondering what the publisher had been doing here and what his last words meant. There was only one way to find out.

"That was the first time I met Mr. Cornell," she said. "He doesn't come in very often?"

"Not very often, no," Natalie said. "He stays mostly in his office over at the commercial printing plant."

"Oh. I see. And why was he wishing you well, Dee? Are you leaving us?"

Maybe that was too bold, but Dee didn't seem upset by her curiosity.

"I will be leaving, but not before Natalie can find a replacement. Mr. Cornell had offered me the opportunity to buy the newspaper and become the publisher, but I decided it wasn't for me. Instead, I think I'll go back to Twin Ports. I have a good home there. It's situated nicely with mountain and water views, a bit secluded. It will be a quiet place for me to write the book that I've always thought about writing."

"Damn. Just when we're getting acquainted, you're leaving. Can't say I'm happy about that myself."

"I won't be going awfully soon, Astrid," Dee said.

"And if you send me an invitation to your housewarming, I will come to it. You can be sure of that."

"Who knows when that'll be. Haven't even started to work much on it yet. I'm just waiting for Abram Lincoln to finish his job at Jake's Hardware. He thinks he'll be through with that job next week."

After supper and six o'clock news, Astrid turned off her small TV. The news about Pete Rose was disturbing, and she reflected once again on reasons she didn't go into pro sports. Unexpected things could happen to shorten a career. Just look at Pete's recklessness in gambling.

"What a damned shame he gambled away his chance at being in the Baseball Hall of Fame," she said. "He belonged there more than a whole lot of others. Oh well. So much for good sense when it comes to an addiction, especially to gambling."

She was about to go upstairs where she was still peeling wallpaper off the third bedroom, when the phone rang. The man calling said he was Jake at the hardware store. Abram's name popped into her mind.

"Ya?"

"Abram Lincoln has been working here for me. He had an unfortunate accident this afternoon, and he wanted me to call you after working hours. He's worried that he won't be able to go onto your job real soon."

"Oh no. How badly is he hurt?

"It's a torn rotator cuff, I understand."

"Where is he? At our hospital?"

"Yes. He did say not to tell you he's in the hospital, but

I decided you'd want to know. He's a very proud man, you know."

"I appreciate that you did tell me. How did it happen?"

"He tried to catch a heavy box, and when he did, he injured his shoulder. I believe he'll be out of commission a very long time, actually."

"I should go to see him. Do you know his room number?"

"It's room three-fourteen. The doctor said he'll need surgery, so he's keeping him quiet before it can be scheduled."

"Thanks for calling me, Jake. You did the right thing to let me know."

The poor man. Astrid recognized that an injury to a carpenter was just as bad as it was for an athlete. Maybe worse, since he wasn't under contract. Now what was she going to do? Should she get another carpenter, or should she just wait until Abram was ready to work again?

She hastily put her daytime pants back on, having changed already to old coveralls, and drove to the hospital where she was directed to his area on the third floor. Before going to Abram's room, she located his attending doctor and asked several questions. Armed with answers concerning the length of time he would be unable to work, Astrid formed a plan as she walked down the hallway toward Abram's open door. She waited a few minutes to think through this plan of hers, and when she was satisfied that it could work, she entered the darkened room.

At first she feared he was unconscious, or maybe dead, he appeared so white. She leaned over and spoke his name.

Without opening his eyes, Abram said, "Doctor, please. I have to go home. I can't afford any more hospital bills. Just give me painkillers to keep going. That's all I need."

"That's for the doctor to decide, not me," Astrid said.

Abram opened his eyes and squinted. Obviously he was heavily sedated.

"What are you doing here?" His words slurred, as if he were drunk. "I told Jake only to say I'd be laid up a few days."

"I know. But I wormed it out of him. What are you saying--you can't afford any more hospital bills. You've been here before?"

He turned his face away. Was it so hard for him to tell her?

"Tell me, Abram. What did you mean by that?"

"It's really not your business. I thought I was talking to the doctor."

"They're going to operate, aren't they?"

"That's what they say." He squinted and groaned in pain despite the drugs. "But I don't want that. I need to work, and I can't if they operate."

Astrid sat in the chair next to his bed, rested an elbow on his nightstand and studied him.

"Looks like you can't anyway, operation or not. How badly are you hurt?"

"Jake's son thought it would be funny to see me try to catch a box full of heavy tiles from the storage loft, but

for thousands of dollars, that money vanished almost overnight."

Astrid frowned.

"Legally, you know, you don't have to pay those bills. They were your brother's, not yours."

A look of shock crossed Abram's face.

"I couldn't do that. It would be like disallowing I had a brother. We were all that were left in my family. How could I not pay his bills? I told him I would when he was in his last days."

Again, she understood. She had done the same thing. Even though no one else in the family helped out, she paid what the insurance company didn't pay on her grandfather's medical bills.

"And he didn't have insurance, I suppose."

"No. He was a builder, like me. Not enough income to take out insurance."

"Well, please allow me to talk with my attorney," she said. "He can help a great deal by writing to all the creditors and offering so much on a dollar in settlement of those bills. Whatever he tells me is the settlement total, I'll take care of. You understand? You no longer need worry about it for now. Some day, if you get on your feet and are able to do it, you can pay me back."

"Wha…? I don't know what to say. Are you crazy?"

"Probably. But I want to have a nice home to live in. I promised myself I would have a place where I could invite friends for dinner or just a pleasant evening of visiting. And I would like to get started on renovations as soon as possible. I was told you are the best carpenter around here, so I'll wait until you can prove it. And I don't want you refusing treatments because you think you can't pay for them. Get it?"

"I get it."

"You won't be able to work for a while. Right?"

"Right."

"So you need a place to live while you're recuperating. I have a plan. You'll stay at my house, and what you can do, that's what you will do. I won't charge you for room and board, but I won't pay you until you can go back to your own house and work full time."

"I only rent a room," he said. "I just don't know what to say. This is overwhelming. I'd ask why, but I can tell that you'll just shrug it off. It's tempting. I'm sure I'll be able to do a few things soon, even with one hand. The damnable thing is that it's the right shoulder that's hurt, and I'm right handed."

He sighed and closed his eyes again. He needed to sleep, and Astrid decided she had given him enough to think about. Most likely it was enough to ease his mind about doing what must be done…getting well.

She tiptoed out the door and down the hallway, smug in the knowledge that she had given someone a bit of hope this day. It's what Grampa would have done. He'd have been proud of her.

SIX
MONDAY, AUGUST 28, 1989

With any luck, Astrid could get Abram home today before she had to be at the office, but experience had taught her that it was unlikely to happen. How many times a doctor pleasantly told her that a loved one could go home tomorrow morning, only to get at the hospital early and then wait until afternoon before the doctor signed a release. She'd give it the good old college try, though, and see if she could find someone with authority to let him go early.

She was anxious to observe Abram's surprise when he saw how she'd set up a place for him in the dining room. She had put in a single bed there, but a nurse told her he wouldn't be able to lie down for quite some time, maybe a month or more. It would be too painful. So she also bought a soft recliner chair, a big one, so he could sleep in it for however long it would take. Since the dining room was next to the kitchen, he would be able to get a snack and cold drink any time he wanted it, and use the powder room off the hallway. She had made several things for him to eat, including her own version of sub sandwiches in small sizes for easy handling.

Standing outside his room, she looked down at what she was wearing. Some day soon she must go shopping for a few new things. Jeans suited her just fine, but neither Natalie nor Dee wore them, and she noticed that they looked her up and down every morning when she entered the office. Oh well. Another day maybe she'd go on that shopping trip.

On entering the room, she found Abram sitting in a chair with the TV on, but asleep. He wore the pajamas and slippers she bought for him, although the right side of the top was draped over the bandaged shoulder. The right arm was held close to his body by a sling.

Astrid noted that his color was better than it was when she saw him Saturday afternoon after his early morning surgery. He barely recognized her before lapsing back into drugged sleep. It had surprised her that the surgeon would perform the operation on a weekend day, but the nurse said it wasn't unusual in emergency cases. She also explained that physical therapy could go on for two, three, or four months, depending on his progress. What a bummer, Astrid thought. An active man who loved his work, incapacitated with very little to do all that time. She didn't even know if he liked to read, but she had put books beside the chair, and now she had a larger TV so that he could play VHS movie tapes. Getting ready for him had taken all her weekend, but he would be more comfortable than as if he went back to a single room with no one to talk with or to help him when he needed it, and nothing to do.

She sat on the edge of the bed, waiting for him to rouse. When she saw a doctor down the hall, she called out to him.

"Doctor. I'd like to see you."

Abram started.

"What is it? What happened?" he mumbled.

"Oh, sorry. Nothing. I just wanted to stop the doctor from getting away."

"That should do it," Abram said.

She was about to go after the doctor, when he came into the room.

"Well," he said, without a trace of emotion. "I see you're ready to leave our hotel. Don't like the service, Abram?"

"Service is fine. The meals stink."

Not knowing the hospital staff, Astrid squinted down at the doctor's name tag.

"Dr. Sahan? Are you the surgeon?"

"I am. Osteopathic surgeon. Are you Mrs. Lincoln?"

"God, no. I'm Astrid Thorpe. I'll be looking after Abram until he can take care of himself."

"You're a nurse, then?"

"No, no. Just a friend."

"A friend. Well, before he goes home, you will need some instructions."

"When do you want to see him again?"

"I'll want to see him in my office in a week. You can stop at the desk and pick up an appointment and an instruction sheet. If things look good in a week, we'll start him on physical therapy."

"When can I pound nails again, Doc?" Abram asked.

"When the physical therapists and I agree that you are

healed enough and have easy movement. And not before that. You had a very large tear. Let it heal thoroughly before you begin strenuous work again."

Dr. Sahan signed the release paper on his clipboard.

"You're all set to go. An aide will be right along to wheel you out to the front door."

As Astrid started to say she would do that, Dr. Sahan held up his hand.

"No objection, now. This is hospital policy."

"I see. Okay. Thanks, doctor. I'm glad to have met you."

"Yes. Good to meet you, too, Miss Thorpe."

Abram sat quietly until the doctor was well out of earshot before speaking.

"Damn. Got to go through physical therapy. That means no knowing how long I'll be out of commission. It's enough to frost your…"

"Never mind," Astrid interrupted. "Be thankful you can go home and that you have good doctors. Just mind your Ps and Qs, and do what they tell you if you want to get back to normal."

"Yes, boss. Whatever you say."

"Make damn sure you remember that--whatever I say. I won't stand for self-pity and complaining in my house. Remember, you're living in my place from now on."

"Hell. This is probably a mistake."

"Suit yourself. When you can walk and do for yourself, then be my guest and go where you want to. But for now, you'll rest and shut up about it."

* * *

Dee was out interviewing a woman who had opened a day school for young children at her home, leaving Natalie and Astrid to cover the office for the rest of the morning. When there was a lull in phone calls, Natalie spoke of Abram.

"How's your patient doing?" she asked.

"Mostly sleeping. Abram told me the pain is the worst he's ever had. It must be bad for a man like that to say he's hurting. He strikes me as a man who would rather die than appear weak."

"I've heard people say the shoulder cuff tear is very bad," Natalie said. "You think it's going to work out, having him in your house while he recuperates?"

"Ya. It will. Right now he's a grumpy, unhappy cuss, but he's determined and he'll get over it, especially when he can start working again. For now, it's just as well to have him there. He had no one to do anything for him in his rented room. I'm going over there later today, after work, and tell the landlady that he's giving up that room."

"What about his things? His clothes and books, whatever?"

"I'll pack them into some boxes that I picked up at the supermarket yesterday. He won't need much for a while. Just getting out of that chair will be hard. I have books for him to read. But you know how it is. When you're on painkillers, you aren't able to concentrate on a book very well."

"That's true enough."

Astrid stood up and walked over to Dee's desk to look out the front window.

"Looking for something?" Natalie said.

"Maybe. The manager at the market said he's a neighbor of the Hollands and Mr. Holland told him yesterday that he's putting his shoe store on the market. Just wanted to see if a For Sale sign had been put up yet. No, I don't see any."

The shoe store was the last shop in the northern Main Street shopping area, across from the newspaper office.

"That's odd," Natalie said. "I was in there last week, and Mr. Holland didn't say anything about it to me. Was he sure of that?"

Astrid shrugged. "Seemed to be."

She was leaning forward, against the windowsill, with one knee bent on Dee's chair.

"Oh, wait a minute. There's a man at the side door. That's it. He's got a sign in his hand. Ya. They're putting it up now."

"That's too bad. I always liked that shoe store. Wonder why he's closing? It's worth your looking into, Astrid. After you finish up there, go over and talk with him. To say the least, a little story in the paper telling of his years of service to the community won't hurt him. I presume he's closing due to retirement."

At noontime, Astrid took a quick trip to Lilac Lane and checked in on Abram, who was sound asleep in his chair. He had been relieved when he came home and saw that he wasn't expected to lie down.

"You have no idea how painful it is to try to get down or up," he told her.

After he worked himself into the chair, he said, "I may never be able to get up."

"I'll give you a hand," Astrid had said then.

Now she watched him for a moment and told herself that bringing him here was the right thing to do. A crease remained between his eyebrows where he had scowled so hard with pain. No doubt, he spent long weeks caring for his brother when he was ill. He deserved a break now.

The sales clerk at the furniture store had promised that the new refrigerator would come no later than Wednesday. She opened this old one to take out a sandwich, and thought that Wednesday wouldn't come too soon to suit her. The inside of it still looked black from mildew even though she had scrubbed it for an hour one day. Everything had to be wrapped or covered tightly to avoid a moldy taste and smell. Abram would wake up and be hungry, so when she had eaten and was ready to go back to the office, she set up a TV stand next to his chair and left a sandwich and glass of water. While he slept on, she studied her guest with interest.

Not the best judge of men, she hoped that she hadn't made a mistake by taking in a perfect stranger, but somehow he didn't appear to be a troublemaker. He had that easy-going way of talking, as if he might say 'Aw, shucks,' at any moment, in a jocular manner like Jimmy Stewart, only with the distinctive downeast cadence. Anyway, right or wrong, she liked Abram from the start, when he asked if he should wipe his feet at the door.

* * *

After parking in *The Bugle* lot, Astrid walked across the street at the intersection, and entered Holland's Shoe Store. She had always associated leather fragrance with men, and loved shopping for shoes mainly for that reason—to breathe in the essence of masculine strength. But today was not a day to fantasize.

"May I help you?" Mr. Holland said as he approached her.

"Maybe, but it's more likely I can help you," Astrid said. "You have a For Sale sign out front. Natalie thought we should write something about it, since you've been in business here for so long."

"Well, that's nice of her. I told the agent to wait on advertising, maybe in a week or two, depending on how it goes."

"How what goes?"

"Oh, you know. The meeting."

"Meeting? What meeting is that?"

"The public meeting."

"Is there a public meeting that I don't know about?"

"There's a notice in the Bangor Sunday paper. Says there's going to be a public hearing on land use in Fairchance Wednesday. I'm surprised you don't know about it."

"What land use are they talking about, Mr. Holland?"

"A farm on the south side of Fairchance. Apparently

they're talking of building a new shopping mall on that property."

A shopping mall! Astrid heard it but couldn't believe it. Not in Fairchance, surely.

"Just where on the south side?"

"Out past the recycle plant. There's a big farm with trees and fields. I think that's what they want a zoning change for."

Astrid felt like a tub of ice water had been dumped over her. The shock of this news hit her all at once, and she envisioned an all-but-secret hearing followed by the sudden appearance of bulldozers knocking down those trees. Next thing, before anyone knew it, construction would be under way and a shopping mall would sprout. If citizens didn't know about the hearing, the project could go through with little or no opposition.

He continued, "Some of us will be forced to close. When a big well-known chain comes in, the small businessman like me can't survive. Who'd buy shoes here for sixty dollars, when they can get them for forty dollars at a chain store that sells maybe a dozen or more pairs to my one pair in a day? I can't compete with that kind of business. I'm trying to get out now before construction begins."

"Don't be too sure about that happening," Astrid said on her way to the door. "Thanks for the heads-up, Mr. Holland."

SEVEN

She went to the business office first to find the advertising copy editor. Astrid nodded to each one as she walked through to the back room, where she found the woman in charge.

"Hi," Astrid said. "You know, I have the memory of a goat when it comes to names. Tell me yours again, please?"

"I'm Willie, short for Wilhelmina. Thank goodness for nicknames, huh?"

"Sometimes."

"Can I help you with something, Astrid?"

"You can tell me whether a legal notice has come in concerning a public Zoning Board hearing this week."

"No, I can tell you it has not. We haven't had any legal notices this week."

"Okay. Thanks, Willie."

Across the hall, she found that Dee had returned and was busy at her computer. Natalie looked up from her desk.

"Did you talk with Mr. Holland?"

Astrid was so excited she couldn't stand still. Pacing from desk to desk, she didn't know where to start. The words came spilling out.

"This is big news. I couldn't believe it. You won't either.

M'god, they've got to be stopped. Fairchance wouldn't be the same."

"Who? What are you talking about?" Natalie asked.

"We haven't had any word come in on it. According to Mr. Holland, there's a legal notice in the *Bangor Sunday Life* announcing a public hearing here in Fairchance concerning a proposed shopping mall. The hearing is Wednesday, he said."

"Are you kidding?" Natalie said. "How could that happen? You're right. We haven't heard anything about it. I wonder if we got a legal notice…"

"I just checked it out. No legal notices this week, Willie said."

Dee shook her head, equally appalled.

"What's going on?" she said. "I thought ours was the newspaper of record for legal notices here."

Natalie said it was. "But a tactic like this, an ad in a Sunday paper, isn't against the law, as long as it is widely distributed in the community. Who reads legal notices in a Sunday newspaper?"

"I'll call the Zoning Board, Natalie." Dee said.

"Yes, you do that. The secretary's name is Randall King. In the meantime, I'll check the Sunday newspaper. I should have caught that, but I didn't read much of the paper this weekend. Anyway, I must admit, I seldom read the legal notices myself."

Astrid went to her desk, feeling helpless while the other two made their phone calls. She wanted to jump in, too, and pull the plug on any big contractor who thought it could just walk into town and start changing the quality of life here.

Dee found the number to call, and dialed. After a few minutes, she began to talk louder.

"So you are going to act on it at this meeting?" Dee asked.

When she got the answer to that question, she pressed further.

"And when were you going to let us know about it? The day after the hearing?"

The answer was brief, and Dee hung up.

"He was going to send over the notice tomorrow morning. It's a company called Construcorp, and an offer has been made on land outside Fairchance. No action has been taken yet. King said they plan to vote on the application for a zoning variance Wednesday night. Who'd have been there if we hadn't found out through the back door? Only those who saw the notice and have an interest in bringing in a mall. Seems like there is some hesitation on the part of the board to get this newspaper involved."

Natalie looked ready to fight King and Construcorp single-handedly.

"Well we're involved now. Astrid, I want you to drop whatever you're doing and take your tape recorder. Go up and down Main Street, talk with as many shop keepers as you can in about two hours then come back and put together their reaction to the news that an application to construct a shopping mall is being acted on by the Zoning Board this week. Be sure not to say the mall is a certainty, only that it's a possibility. And don't forget to use the tape recorder. I want everyone to be quoted word for word, as accurately as possible. Include some from those who may want the project to go forward, people like attorneys, bankers, insurance agents. They might see a mall as a blessing for their interests. We want to have an across-the-board mix of reaction."

Astrid began clearing her desk while Natalie continued.

"Dee, write up a story that tells about the track record for shopping centers. You know as well as I do what the big ones are--those that have whole malls sitting with decaying vacant stores because they've either gone out of business or moved to newer malls. And be sure to cite the downtown blight they cause as stores close. Call anyone you can think of anywhere in the state who will warn against moving business out of town to a mall."

She got to her feet and looked out the window at Main Street.

"Of all the underhanded--they'd probably have held that board hearing without any citizens present, and all of a sudden we'd have been sitting here with egg on our faces for not having informed the public about what was happening. If they got it approved secretly, then the damned contractor could get the construction under way."

She thought for a few seconds.

"I'll run out to the property myself and take a look, get some photos of the area. And when I come back, I'll write an editorial."

She sat down and took her camera bag out of the desk.

"One thing we don't want to do is accuse anyone of cover-up. We may think that, and I can make an editorial hint at secrecy, but what we really want to do is stir up voters to get to that meeting."

Astrid was at the door, ready to do her interviews.

"I'll urge everyone to be there," she said, and left the room.

This was what she'd been waiting for, a chance to be in a good fight for a cause. Heading down Main Street, Astrid felt more energized than she ever did entering a basketball game. The thought of the stores on this wonderful Main Street going to blight because of a tinsel town mall made this assignment feel like a real mission, to say nothing of a good fight. She wondered what the board meeting would be like after *The Bugle* hit the streets tomorrow afternoon. She'd be there. And if they needed a voice against approval of the project, she would speak out.

Her first stop was at the town's Five and Dime store. Prices had gone up since its opening many years ago, but the name remained the same and goods were still reasonable. She found the manager in the office, an elevated room with a glass window where the manager watched shoppers. The door sign announced the manager as Wm. Lytle. She found him standing by a water cooler, drinking from a cylindrical paper cup.

"Mr. Lytle?" she asked, when the door opened to her knock.

"Yes. May I help you?"

She introduced herself and told him about the proposed shopping mall. The man sat down, his wood swivel chair squeaking as if it were tired. He waited behind the wood desk while she sat in a straight chair facing him.

"We're trying to ascertain how local business owners and managers would react to this proposal," Astrid said. "Do you have a comment to make, Mr. Lytle?"

"We've kept those robbers out of here for years. They'd better not think they can come in and roll over us now. I'll be one voice against this skullduggery. You can bet money on that. Fairchance isn't going to be turned into a ghost town to make big merchants rich outside our gates. There are plenty of malls that our people can drive to as it is, if that's the kind of shopping they want to do. But nothing can replace the family-owned businesses that we have."

He sat forward and raised his chin.

"Does that answer your question?"

"I think it does, sir. And I thank you for being candid."

His words were echoed all along Main Street, and even at a few smaller shops that she visited off the main drag. One was a gun shop, where the sixty-plus owner tapped her arm to emphasize his words.

"I own this place and have for thirty years. There's no way I can afford to rent one of those shops. I wouldn't, anyway. I have men and women come here from all around. This may look like so much junk to you, but collectors and hunters paw through it to find something that's a real treasure to them. If our city guardians give the contractors a green light, they'll find themselves out of a job come next election. I'll guarantee the public hearing will not be peaceful."

Astrid took the comments and her notes to the office. She worked into the evening until nine o'clock, along with Dee and Natalie. By the time they were all finished with their stories, they knew the newspaper this week would be well read, and that the hearing room would need more than a few extra chairs at Wednesday's meeting.

* * *

So intense had the effort been that Astrid forgot about her guest until she walked into the house and saw him standing in the kitchen doorway.

"Oh, hell," she said. "I'm sorry I'm so late, Abram. Are you okay? You look white. Shouldn't you be resting?"

"No. I'm fine. Just about to scare up a bite to eat."

"We've had such a day. You wouldn't believe. I'll get something quick and easy, if it's okay with you. How about bacon and scrambled eggs? Can you believe it, the Zoning Board was going to meet Wednesday night and act on a land use proposal that has been filed by a contractor who builds shopping malls. It's supposed to be a public hearing, but they never gave us a word on it. They put the legal notice in Sunday's newspaper, and only by chance did I find out about it when I interviewed Mr. Holland. You know, the shoe store owner. He put up a For Sale sign and I went over thinking I'd be writing a story about his retirement. He said he's trying to sell before too many know about the mall, and I told Natalie. Well, we found out it was true and that the hearing is going to be held Wednesday. The public wouldn't have known anything about it until it was too late. But they'll know about it now. You wait until you see the paper tomorrow."

"Hey, take a breath. You're wired. Better just slow down, Astrid. A shopping mall, huh?"

She held up the frying pan and gave him a questioning look. He nodded.

"Yeah, bacon and eggs are fine," he said. "You don't think a mall would be such a good idea?"

Astrid wrinkled her nose.

"No way. Do you?"

"It would give me some work, and others like me. Mall construction isn't done overnight. I'd be happy enough about it, to have a good winter's work. And the wages are always high on those jobs,"

Astrid said nothing until the bacon began to sizzle. She turned down the gas burner flame, trying to contain her anger at Abram's view of the mall idea.

"I guess I thought you'd be fairly busy here this winter," she said.

"Who knows? To say the least, this job won't last for too many weeks, once I can work again."

He fell against the counter. Reaching out to steady himself with his left hand, he knocked over a tumbler.

"You don't look so good," Astrid said. "Sit down. Food's about ready."

"Whew. I don't feel so good, either. Those pills are strong."

"Go back to your chair. I can bring a plate and put it on a TV tray."

"Yeah. Thanks. I'll do that."

"Need a hand?"

"I can make it okay."

By the time Astrid had everything ready, she found Abram asleep again. This time she woke him. He needed food. She said no more about the mall, but his attitude gave her an uneasy feeling since there would be others who felt the same as he did. Natalie had already pointed out the professionals who would stand to gain by such a project, and Astrid had talked with a couple of them who expressed an indifferent attitude. She had no idea how many were unemployed in Fairchance, but there had to be plenty from surrounding towns who would want a construction job. Her hope was that enough naysayers would be at the meeting Wednesday to convince the board members not to approve the zoning change.

EIGHT
WEDNESDAY, AUGUST 30, 1989

At noon, Natalie told Dee and Astrid to go home for the afternoon, and to join her at the hearing tonight. They were all anxious about the turnout and what the balance of sentiment would be.

"We all need to relax for now," Natalie said. "We've done all we can for the present. So just take it easy this afternoon. Meet me five or ten minutes before seven,"

Before going home, Astrid went to the Register of Deeds office for a bit of research, and then she shopped for groceries. She arrived home just after one o'clock and picked up her mail from the mailbox at the sidewalk. Two bills and a hardware store sales flyer were typical of what she ever received, but it was her own fault, not being one to write letters herself. It followed that her few friends at a distance were discouraged from writing to her. Some day she would sit down and write to several friends all at once. Christmas would be a good time to do it.

She looked closer at the envelopes and found that one was not a bill, but a letter addressed to Mrs. Guilford. In the kitchen, she found Abram sitting at the table, reading from a spiral-bound notebook, while spread around on the table were desk items--papers, envelopes, greeting cards.

"You look better," she said. "How are you feeling?"

"Not good, but I had to get out of that chair. And that wasn't easy."

"What are you doing?" Astrid asked.

"I thought I'd clean out the kitchen desk. It was full of stuff. This is as far as I got."

"That's nice of you," she said. "I received a letter that's addressed to Mrs. Guilford. Wonder what I should do with it."

"Just forward it."

"But, if it's advertising, which seems likely, they won't forward it anyway."

"Does it look like advertising?"

"I'm not sure. There's no return address, and I don't know what her address is. The real estate agent thought she was in a Bangor nursing home."

"If it's a worry to you, then open the thing."

Astrid raised an eyebrow, but put the letter on the desk. She would never open another person's mail. She needed to find the woman's current address and get it to her.

"I found something that may interest you, since you're a writer," Abram said. He held up the notebook.

"Ya? What is it?"

"Not quite sure. It starts out with a title, *The Good Man*. And the author's name is Doris Guilford."

"Something she left behind. I wonder why she didn't take it with her."

"I guess she was writing a novel. That's why I began reading it. I didn't think it would matter now that you own the house and all that's in it. So, obviously it isn't secret, or she wouldn't have left it. The more I read, the more interested I got and forgot the time."

"What's it about?"

"It's written in first person. I don't know what to think of it. Like I said, I thought it was the start of a novel, but the way it's written, I'm not so sure. It's the story of a woman who marries a man, thinking he's one thing, and he turns out to be something other than she thought he was. Listen to how it starts out:

"Everyone told me how good this man was. He was a faithful church member and a Boy Scout leader. They said he was wealthy, didn't drink, and didn't chase women. My father knew him, and he told me to accept his offer of marriage. I would be happy with this good man, he said. He told me that I would never get another offer as good, if any at all. I thought he was probably right."

Abram looked up and Astrid gave him a smile, but she really wasn't interested in something Mrs. Guilford left behind when she went to the nursing home. Maybe the woman realized she could never sell a minor manuscript even if she got back home and sent it out to publishers. She could only think about the hearing ahead. The energy she had put into reporting about it and the mental preparation for tonight were difficult to suppress, even now. If she didn't busy herself she'd be tearing her hair out.

"Funny thing," Abram said, "she doesn't identify him right away. Of course, I haven't read very far."

"I wonder if it's finished. Doesn't look very long for a novel. Maybe it's intended to be a short story, instead."

"It's tightly written by hand, so there's more than you think here. You might want to read some of it when you get a chance."

Astrid noted how he held his left hand over the right arm. He must be in pain, but here he was, trying to do something helpful.

"Are you sure you're okay?" she asked.

"Not too bad."

"You know you mustn't do too much for a while. You'll be starting physical therapy soon. You don't want to do something that would cause you to have to be operated on again."

His look said she had just stated the obvious, but Astrid knew she would have to be strong with him. She'd had a stubborn patient before.

She brought their soup and sandwiches to the table and again asked if he needed help.

"No. I can manage," he said.

His left-handed work was so sloppy that she wanted to help. However, she remained silent and let him get through his lunch the best way he could. Soup wasn't all that hard to clean up, after all.

"Why don't you read the manuscript each day and tell me about it when I come home?" Astrid said.

"Are you home for the day?"

"No. Just a few hours. I'm going to the hearing tonight."

"Oh yes. The shopping mall. I'd like to go."

Astrid almost blurted that he damned well better not,

but she thought that might be too commanding on her part.

"You think you're up to it?" she asked.

"Not really. I still get nauseous when I'm on my feet. I'll just wait for a report from you."

If she had told him he shouldn't attend, he might have tried anyway. Amazing how reverse psychology worked. Astrid felt smug as she thought about it.

"I'll scrape the rest of that wallpaper off the living room wall this afternoon, since I have a few hours," she said. "If you want to, you can come in and read to me. I'd like to hear it."

After they finished eating, Astrid cleared the table and then filled a pan with water to soak what paper wouldn't peel easily. Abram followed her to the living room.

"Wait a minute," she said. "Let me get you a chair. A kitchen chair okay?"

"Sure."

She carried a chair to the center of the room, and put it down facing her. After he sat down, and while she dabbed water on the stuck paper, he began to read aloud:

"I believed with all my heart that I would be happy with him, especially when I saw the lovely house he had built for us. My family had a farmhouse, miles from here. I had not known the luxury of running water or of an indoor bathroom. As a schoolgirl I walked a mile to the one-room schoolhouse. My clothes were all made by my mother or passed down from a neighbor's oldest daughter, and when I learned to sew, I made all that I wore. I worked in the fields, cut hay with a hand scythe.

I milked two cows, morning and night. I carried water from the spring in the woods behind our house twice a day. The days were long and tiring. I was happy to marry a man who would take me away from the drudgery."

Astrid had stopped scraping to listen.

"I grew up on a farm," she said, "but I didn't have to work like that, unless I wanted to. I was happy, but only because I enjoyed sharing work with the men. Sounds like that poor girl was forced to work like a slave."

"That's what I'm thinking, too."

"We had a real nice home with modern appliances and running water. My grandfather had a large farming enterprise, with lots of help."

Abram moaned and grabbed his shoulder.

"You're hurting," Astrid asked. "You want to go back to the recliner?"

"No, I'll read a bit more. You have a lot to do there yet. Why don't you use the scraper instead of your fingernails?"

"I do most of the time. But sometimes it's just easier to get a nail under it and flick it off."

He grunted, but didn't offer more advice.

"You planning to paper or paint these walls?"

"I like wallpaper, but painting is less of a problem when it has to be done over. What do you think?"

He looked surprised that she asked him.

"I like paint myself."

She would have painted it whatever his opinion was, but it seemed to her that by asking him for an opinion, he might feel like he was being useful instead of just living here like an unwanted boarder.

"Then I think I'll paint it white so I can put any color with it."

He studied the room and then nodded approvingly. With his left hand, he raised the notebook once again and continued:

"We had a quiet wedding ceremony. Just my father and mother and two family friends and a small reception at my parents' house, and I changed to a new daytime dress to go to his house.

"It took two and a half hours to get here. He was quiet for about fifteen minutes, so I thought to break the ice by speaking of how good the cake was. He said cake was cake. And that was that. I didn't try again to make conversation and I wondered why he was so sullen. He was always pleasant enough when he called on me and he acted real pleased at the wedding reception. Now he was silent. His eyes looked glazed.

"We arrived at the house and I was so excited to have a house to call my own. Everything seemed romantic and dream-like. The house was beautiful. It looked like a castle to me. The lawn and the flower beds were all neat and pretty. Grass was dark green and the house was white instead of the old gray house and dried up grass that I'd come from.

"I walked ahead of him into the house and just stood admiring everything. Marble top tables were so pretty. I ran to the kitchen and turned on a faucet. I was fascinated by running water.

"My husband remained silent. He went back to the car and brought in my one suitcase. Then he said he was going upstairs and told me to follow him up."

Astrid noticed that Abram's voice was becoming strained. The pain was too much. He was trying too hard to overcome, and it was her fault for having been bossy and bringing him here. If he'd gone somewhere else, maybe he'd have taken it easy and let himself heal.

"I'm sorry, but that's as far as I can read for now," he said. "I guess I will go to my chair and relax for a while."

"Just when the story is getting interesting," Astrid said. "I'm joking, of course. We can continue another day. I have to start supper now, so I can get ready for the hearing. Do you want a pain pill now?"

"Yes, thanks. It's funny, isn't it. The story has no names and no location. I can't tell if it's fact or fiction."

"That is funny. Guess we'll find out later. She had a fairly good command of English. Doesn't sound like an uneducated country girl. I'm interested to know what happens to her."

NINE

The parking lot was nearly full when Astrid arrived. She had to walk from the far end to the Court House door, and when she entered, she found the lobby crowded with noisy voters waiting for the hearing room doors to be opened. Natalie and Dee spotted her first and called her name.

"Wow," Astrid said on approaching the two. "I never expected to see this many people turn out. What do you think the mood of the crowd is?"

"From what people around us are saying," Natalie said, "I'd say the consensus is that no one wants a shopping mall near our city. Of course, we've only heard a few talking."

"Do we stay together or cover separate points in the room?" Dee asked.

"Split up. That way we'll get different photo angles and we can talk with those sitting around us. And both of you remember, don't be afraid to speak up if you think something that's said isn't right. If they make a statement of fact, question how they reached that conclusion. Hold them responsible for their words and actions. Most of all, it's important for them to listen to what the voters want. Okay?"

Astrid and Dee agreed just as the doors opened. The crowd grew quiet, walked inside, and picked their favorite positions in the room. Astrid went to the right, Natalie marched down to the front row, and Dee wandered over to the left side. Inside, the volume of discussions began to increase, but it didn't drown out loud coughing, sneezing, and nose-blowing throughout the room. The rampant spread of summer colds this year worried Astrid. She hoped she wouldn't take a cold bug home to Abram. He was suffering enough without a cold.

On the stroke of seven o'clock, two women and three men walked in from a side door and sat at desks facing the audience. Along the wall, at the left of the desks, was a row of chairs, where three men in dark business suits took their places. As soon as they were seated, the audience fell silent again, except for the coughing spasms, and the steady click of the schoolhouse clock.

At an angle between audience and Zoning Board members, an easel promised a peek at the Fairchance Mall Plan, according to the cover sheet title.

The man at the center desk looked up and said, "Good evening. Nice to see so many public-spirited citizens here tonight. We usually have no need for more than half a dozen chairs. Well."

Astrid thought, from the man's disgruntled manner, that he probably would have preferred seeing only a half dozen here tonight. Knowing that she was in large part responsible for this turnout, she felt pride welling up and fluttering the corners of her lips. It wasn't every day that a reporter stumbled onto a really big story that upset sneaky politicians. She hoped citizens would speak out against the zoning change.

"I'm Randall King," the man said, "secretary of the Fairchance Board of Zoning Appeals. To my right are Pat Anderson and Bruce Roberts. At my left are Marianne Knox and Lionel Hanson. The three men by the wall over there are Mr. Carney, Mr. Matthau, and Mr. Kirkland, all representing Construcorp. The company has filed an application for a land variance on The Plains Road. The request is for a zoning change from rural residential and farming district to commercial."

Local politicians tended not to be overly articulate, Astrid thought, while she remembered the college leadership and how they gloried in words of at least three syllables, often leaving the audience lingering over a sentence and missing the punch line. There was a lot to be said for simple sentences.

Secretary King read the details of the application, and held up forms and sketches as he described each one and assured the audience that a plot plan and floor plan had been duly filed, thus meeting the ordinance requirements.

As soon as he finished and looked up, Natalie was on her feet.

"Natalie Burke of *The* Bugle," she said.

"We know who you are, Mrs. Burke. You have a question?"

"Yes. Has Construcorp purchased this property?" she asked.

"No, not yet, Mrs. Burke, but…"

"Then the company has an option to purchase?"

Secretary King looked from side to side at members of

the board. He appeared to be uneasy, picking up papers, tapping them into even packs and laying each one on the desk again.

"We haven't had time..." King stopped, obviously catching himself before divulging more than he thought he should.

Beckoning to one of the three men at the side, he said, "Mr. Carney, would you care to respond to that question?"

Carney rose from his chair, and continued to study a sheaf of papers in his hands. Astrid decided that these men thought holding papers looked quite official and that no one in the audience could understand the masterful wisdom contained in those documents. Either that, or they were nervous on the hot seat. Her opinion of paper shufflers was never top shelf.

Finally, after keeping everyone waiting a full minute, he looked over the heads of all those in the room. His face held a sneer that would have done Clint Eastwood proud.

"An agreement has been reached, ladies and gentlemen. Needless to say, this enterprise will greatly benefit the citizens of your fair city."

Natalie took advantage of his pause before he could say more.

"Does that mean you actually have made a purchase offer, that you have a monetary binder on the property, Mr. Carney?"

Astrid could imagine his quick draw before shooting

her. If he'd said, "Make my day," his expression couldn't have been more menacing.

"We are in agreement with the owner of the property."

"You are in verbal agreement or do you have a binding agreement?"

"Mrs...Burke, is it? I am the president of Construcorp, and I assure you this company has an outstanding record of reliability, honesty, and credit. When we give our word..."

"We're not interested in your reliability, honesty, or credit, and certainly not your word, no matter how outstanding it all may be, Mr. Carney. We submit that if you have no deed and no option to purchase the property, then the citizens have every right to be heard and to block your proposed construction here in Fairchance, if that is their wish."

She turned dramatically to the crowd and a loud shout of assent filled the room, until the secretary's gavel struck several times, and everyone finally settled down.

"Let me remind you, Mrs. Burke," Secretary King said, "this board makes its own decision concerning approval or disapproval of the zoning change. We will now hear about the proposal. That's what we are assembled for, and I expect that everyone will give Mr. Carney the courtesy of being heard. So, Mr. Carney, please continue."

Carney took his place beside the easel and flipped over the top page.

"This is how the mall entrance will appear. It is to be a theme mall with a children's play area that includes a merry-go-round and other rides and games. As you see, we will provide an arched entrance with the appearance of a Ferris wheel. And, in keeping with the theme, we propose that it be called The Wonderland Shopping Center."

Now a man, in gray flannel shirt despite the heat of the night, stood up at the back of the room.

"And just what will a zoning change mean to this city? Is Wondaland where we'll be while you're picking our pockets?"

Everyone laughed and he continued to hold the floor.

"All that fertile land that used to grow wheat and corn for a producing dairy farm would be paved and every tree would be ground up and dumped. Is that the way the wind blows, Mistah Cahney?"

Mr. Carney walked to the center of the room, in front of the board members' desks. He extended his chin in an attitude of, 'Go ahead. Take a swing.'

"You *are* right, sir."

Murmurs rippled through the crowd. Mr. Carney held up his hand for quiet and continued.

"Construcorp will come in, clear the land, and build you an attractive shopping center. We'll plant new trees and shrubbery, and provide a place where you can shop at popular stores like JC Penney, Sears, Hallmark. We'll even create a food court, and other food vendors may set up in the complex. Best of all, it will be within a couple of miles from your fair city. A community's tax base benefits from one of our shopping malls. Jobs are created for people from miles around. In short, it is one of the best improvements this city will ever make."

The farmer was still standing, with his hands in his twill pants.

"Well, now, that's a mighty slick presentation, Mistah Cahney. And what happens to our downtown stores? How many o' them will close because of your populah stores out there? What about people who don't drive and like to walk downtown to shop and visit?"

"A shopping mall, sir, does not have to be the death knell for a city. Most of the stores will remain open. Maybe a few stores operating at a borderline profit will close. But invariably those shoppers who can't drive find ways to get to a mall. They walk and visit there just like on Main Street."

By now, voices were being raised all over the room.

"We're not Alice. Take your Wonderland and disappear."

"Keep it out," one man shouted.

"Fairchance doesn't want a concrete jungle, mister."

"We don't want you here."

"I do," a woman screamed. "I want the option of going to a shopping mall without driving thirty-five miles."

"Move there, then, so you don't have to drive."

"Yeah. You can get junk jewelry here at the five and dime just as well as at a mall."

A man, whom Astrid recognized as the owner of the gun shop, rose and held up a hand for silence. His hoarse voice was evidence of another summer cold.

"We know what happens to city downtown areas,"

he said. "When a mall goes in, Main Street becomes a ghost town of empty shops. We also know that some malls become obsolete when another contractor puts up a new one. Then the first mall is nothing more than empty stores, and a great big eyesore just like Main Street. No one wins. No one."

The crowd again loudly agreed, more shouts went up.

"Go away."

"What are the taxpayers paying for this?"

"Yeah. How much will it cost us in the end?"

Things were getting out of hand, and the secretary again pounded his gavel several times. A man, sitting three seats from Natalie in the front row, stood and waited to be recognized by the secretary.

"Yes. Mr. Oberlin. You have something to say?"

"I do, Mr. Secretary."

Carney returned to his seat.

Oberlin turned to face the audience. He studied faces, one by one, row by row, and then began his oration. The drop of a pin would have echoed in the silence.

"As most of you know, I am Hugh Oberlin, the interim mayor of Fairchance."

Astrid had not seen the man before now, but she had heard Natalie and Dee speak of him following his appointment. Obviously they described him quite accurately, from his size forty-five waistline to his triple chins, and, most weird of all, bare head on top but long hair in back pulled into a pony tail.

"My interest in this proposed project is two-fold," he said. "First, the welfare of our working people."

He sounded like he was the father of the city, Astrid thought. Our working people? Whose? His and the board members? After all, he said himself that he was only the interim mayor.

"Those of you who will help build the mall will be able to provide your families with wages and benefits that you haven't seen before in Fairchance. You will have a forty-hour work week, with evenings and weekends to spend with your families. When the project is completed, you will take great pride in the fact that you were one of the people who built such a fine center for the community."

Oberlin did not wait for anyone to comment, though several hands went up in a now-subdued effort to be heard.

"Secondly, those women, yes and men, too, who will work in the new shops will likewise receive wages to be proud of. No more working for less than minimum wage. Everyone will be paid handsomely at this most unique mall."

Astrid noticed the black suits ducking their heads.

"But there is one other point I'd like to make. The fact that Construcorp has not yet completed its purchase of the land is really insignificant. They will do so, and will be true to their word in all aspects of the upcoming construction. I can assure you of that because I have personally gone to great lengths to investigate the company. I've seen shopping centers that they have built, and every one is unique and operating to full capacity.

I say to you tonight, fellow citizens, do not be alarmed by negatives that you've heard or read, nor afraid to hop onto the prosperity wagon. This is an opportunity that you must embrace and endorse."

Wow. Astrid heard the murmurs and sounds of doubt creeping into listeners' minds. But she knew something that apparently few others knew, and since no one else had brought it up, she would. Standing, she pulled herself to her full height and projected her voice from the diaphragm.

"Mr. Secretary," she said.

Still standing, Oberlin closely scrutinized her before he sat down, while the room hushed as if being led by a music conductor.

"I am Astrid Thorpe of *The Bugle* staff. I have a question for any one of you on the board who wishes to answer it. Will you tell us, please, who is the current owner of the land in question?"

The members of the board whispered among themselves, so Astrid repeated her question.

"Come now, it can't be that difficult. Is it not true that the owner of that land is one of you board members? Mr. King?"

"Well," he said, clearing his throat several times. "As it happens, yes, I do own the land."

"Well, I'll be damned," Astrid said and the crowd laughed. "Now, I thought that just a few weeks ago a woman by the name of Christine Wolf, whose husband died three months ago, was the sole owner of that property."

From the other side of the room, "Yeah. Chris owned that farm."

Again, the crowd hummed and several coughed.

"Well. Well." King was stuttering. "I decided to buy it from her. But…"

Murmurings continued throughout the room.

"But I would not have voted on the variance. As I said before, the application papers are all in order, and…"

"But," Astrid interrupted, "without even an option to buy, you are not obligated to act in favor of the project. And it's apparent that there is a conflict of interest on the Zoning Board. Taken together it would appear that positive action to this variance would be out of line, to say nothing of getting the cart before the horse. Perhaps you should take a poll of the voters and find out how many want to have a shopping mall at their back door."

The shouts convinced King that he should do just that, and when a show of hands left only half a dozen not voting against the project, he announced that the board members thanked all those present for their input.

"We'll adjourn and reconvene in one week to vote on whether to issue a variance to Construcorp."

King slammed the gavel one last time and rushed out the side exit, followed by all the board members and the men in black from Construcorp.

Astrid found herself surrounded by an admiring group of citizens ready to congratulate her for an outstanding job of putting the board to heel. Natalie and Dee pushed through the throng and joined her.

When they were all outside again, Natalie asked, "How

did you know about that land sale, Astrid? How did you think of looking it up? I found out there was no sale or lease, but I never thought that there might be conflict of interest involved."

"I had some dealings with land sharks when I helped my brother after our grandfather died. After the board's secrecy in advertising the hearing, I decided I should do a bit of title searching. Our Mr. King must have seen a chance to make a bundle by buying that land Mrs. Wolf owned."

"You certainly pulled the rabbit out of the hat,"

Astrid was beginning to feel giddy. She'd done a good job and had the praise of her boss. Not a bad day's work, all in all. She grinned.

"Secretary King did a helluva shrinking act, didn't he?"

"He certainly did," Dee said.

They all had a good laugh, but Natalie pointed out that it wasn't over yet. The next time they'd meet, the board would be prepared. They couldn't ease up on this issue. The newspaper would need to apply more aggressive pressure to keep the public's interest up and not let the project go through simply because residents thought they had won over the board tonight.

For her part, Astrid thought she had already outdone herself. What could she possibly do to top it, or be better prepared for the almost certain sentiment of the board members to allow Construcorp to bring its sprawling mall to Fairchance? She hoped that Natalie and Dee would come up with a plan of attack.

TEN

The house was still very warm, even at nine thirty, and Astrid found Abram where he was when she left, his head laid back and the fan set on high, its cooling breeze flowing over his body. In his hand was the open notebook. Obviously he fell asleep reading the manuscript, if that's what it should be called.

Since he couldn't put his arm through the sleeve of a shirt yet, he had to wear it with one arm in and the other sleeve draped over his shoulder. He had managed to get out of the one sleeve and was sitting bare from the waist up.

Not one to get excited over the male body, Astrid nevertheless watched him for a few minutes before speaking his name. She found it interesting that his strong biceps were outlined by a demarcation line of dark tan over the lower arms. Odd that he didn't take off his shirt when he worked outdoors. Her brother always took his off so that he'd have an even tan all over after the inevitable initial burn of the season. Well, she thought, maybe Abram wasn't as vain as Gunnar.

"You awake, Abram?" she said when he stirred a bit.

"Wha…? Oh, yeah, yeah. I'm awake. What time is it, anyway?"

"A little after nine-thirty. You hungry?"

"No, I'm fine. How did the hearing go?"

"It went well. At least from my viewpoint it went well. Not so sure about the construction company's take on it, though, or the Zoning Board's. You wouldn't believe the crowd. And they were definitely not friendly Indians, I'll tell you."

Holding his right arm to his body, Abram sat up straighter. Astrid turned the only other chair in the room, a swivel, so that she could face him while she detailed the meeting. When she finished relating how she challenged the secretary concerning the ownership of the property, Abram laughed.

"You did that? Good for you. You're a contender, Astrid. What did King say to that?"

"He just sort of wilted. He knew they were in quicksand, and they couldn't act on the variance with the crowd all in an uproar. But Dee and Natalie think next week's meeting may bring a reversal of tonight's inaction. That board definitely wants to bring the shopping center to Fairchance, and I don't know how we'll stop them."

"Seems to me you already have done that. No company is going to buck popular sentiment as strong as they found here tonight, Astrid. I saw it over in Castleton, near the coast. Citizens picketed and attended the hearings, until the builders just packed up their briefcases and walked away."

"Really? Well, maybe we'll have some luck after all."

Then she thought how much the work would mean to Abram and others like him. In reality, a project like that would bring a bit more prosperity to the region, but she hoped Fairchance wouldn't fall into the same trap that so many cities had.

"I'm sorry, Abram. I know how much the work would mean to you. But we have such a lovely community here. So few cities have remained the same after a big mall took over. I can think of only a couple that retained their downtown character."

"Hey. You do your thing and don't worry about me, Astrid. You do what you think is right. I have to agree on that point. Shopping malls often do more harm than good. And if their stores don't get the business they need to survive, then the owners close and walk away. I'm on the fence about this one. As I said, don't worry about me. I could use the work, but I have to live here in Fairchance, too, and I want what's best for the community."

Astrid reached over and patted his arm. It was best to drop the issue for now, since he was being so agreeable. She reached for the TV Guide and flipped to the current day.

"Did you watch any TV tonight?"

"No. I read until I got sleepy."

"Ah. The mysterious manuscript. Anything of interest?"

"Yeah, as a matter of fact. This man was a brute. Here, I'll let you read it. I'm too weary now to read any more. Start here."

He turned back a few pages and said, "This is where we left off. He had just demanded that she go upstairs with him."

"Oh, yeah. Want me to read aloud?" she asked.

"No, I've read several pages beyond that. And I'm feeling very tired."

He leaned back again and closed his eyes. He would soon be in drugged sleep, no doubt the best thing for him right now.

"Just take it easy and go to sleep," Astrid said. "I'll go upstairs and read this in bed. I need something to calm me down before I sleep anyway."

* * *

After a bath, Astrid put on clean pajamas, brushed out her long hair, and propped herself on two pillows atop the bed. Night air coming through the window was cooling slightly, and she felt comfortable and happy. Reaching for the spiral notebook, she thought how nice it was to be a homeowner, even if it was a house that needed so much renovation. There was something to be said for having a man in the house, too, even if he couldn't fight his way out of a paper bag. Just his presence made her feel safe.

She opened to the page where Abram indicated she should begin reading and found the following:

"I began to be afraid when I got to the bedroom. Nobody said what to expect. My mother only told me he would be kind to me, and that was all I needed to know. If she had told me everything I would have been a little more at ease. He did not seem kind when he faced me beside the bed. He scowled and told me to take off my clothes. I had never done that in front of anyone as an adult, and it made me scared. I understood that I should do what my husband told me to do, but he had not held me or kissed me like I expected he would. I thought being married meant we would cuddle up and talk. He had kissed me when he proposed and at the wedding. Now what would happen, I didn't know. He stood there looking fierce. I fumbled with the buttons so he would see how nervous I was.

"He took his shirt off and threw it on the floor. He started to unbutton his trousers, and I started to cry. I wanted to run away but I had no place to go. He said I was his wife and a wife's duty was to do what her husband wanted. All I could do was stand there and cry. I was terrified. He grabbed me to him and ripped my dress off. The buttons flew all over the floor. I had made that dress by hand. It broke my heart to see it torn apart like that.

"By the time he had all my clothes off me, I was shaking and sobbing harder. I begged him not to do any more. Since I did not know what he intended to do, I could only believe that he meant to hurt and humiliate me. I was right.

"It's too painful to remember that night. When he got atop me and plunged into me, I felt like I'd been ripped apart inside, just like he tore my dress, and I told him he was hurting me, but he kept on. I was thankful when it ended, and I got up to go clean myself in the bathroom. But he wasn't asleep. He told me to stay where I was. I tried to explain that I was bloody and needed to wash, but he wouldn't let me leave. So I tried to rest as best I could. I guess I fell asleep. Suddenly I felt his weight on me again, and I said, Oh no, please don't. But he did. This time it pained me even more, like a knife cutting in the same wounds. It seemed to please him to hear me cry. He finally went to sleep and I crept out of the room to clean up. The blood scared me for I was sure I would die."

Astrid stopped reading, unable to go on.

"That rotten bastard," she said. "It will be a cold day in hell before a man does that to me. I'd tear *him* apart, starting with the first handle I could find on him."

She rested her head on the pillows, picturing the pitiful state of a newlywed woman who knew nothing about sex and fully trusted her husband to be gentle with her, only to be raped.

Astrid thought, "She didn't even know what that assault was called. Well, if this is a novel, it's quite wrenching, but I still doubt a publisher would take it as it is."

Reading usually calmed her down, but the nature of this manuscript riled her temper instead, and she lay awake for several minutes thinking about the differences in people, especially men. She recalled the first boy who tried to fondle her as a teenager. They had gone fishing together and were sitting by a brook out back of the Thorpe farm, when he suddenly reached out and grabbed her breast and planted a kiss, just short of her lips. She swung her bent right arm around and hit him in the solar plexus. He doubled over and gagged a couple of times. Before he fled, he gave her a look that suggested he likely would not go fishing with her again.

The next young man, however, was different. He was a senior and she was a junior in high school. He talked very softly of love and the pleasures of love-making, until she decided to give it a try. Unlike the bride in the manuscript, Astrid found the whole experience quite pleasant. However, like most teenage flings of that sort, it was soon forgotten when he went to college and she devoted all her spare time to basketball.

A noise outside startled her back to the present. She looked toward the window and listened. Nothing. This wasn't the first time she'd heard strange noises out there. Maybe she should go downstairs and investigate. Still, she didn't want to wake Abram. All this sleeping he did was aiding him to heal. Next week he would see the surgeon and find out when he would begin physical therapy. She decided to wait until tomorrow morning, and then take a look around the shed area. It could be an animal prowling around. Or it could be a human prowler, but what would anyone be snooping around that old shed for? She hadn't looked around much, but there were mostly old hand tools that no one would be interested in today, as far as she knew.

She relaxed and again thought about the words she had just read. If this turned out to be a diary, instead of a novel or short story, then it would mean that Mrs. Guilford was telling about her own horrifying experience. That would be too sad. Since everyone knew that truth was stranger than fiction, it was possible that this was the truth. But why would the woman leave it behind when she vacated the house? It would make more sense to keep it with her, especially if she didn't want prying eyes to read it. Ah. Maybe that was it. Maybe she *did* want someone to find and read it. But why? To edit it and try to sell the story? To make it known to the community that her husband was a brute?

Curiosity got the best of her, and Astrid picked up the notebook and read on:

"I didn't die, but sometimes I wished I had. The first six months of marriage were a nightmare to me. I never knew when he would attack me in bed, and I began to stay up later than he did with the pretense that I wanted to finish a book I was reading. It did not work for long. He started his old way of yelling at me to get to bed again, and I obeyed. One night I didn't go right up when he called. He came running down the stairs and into the living room. He grabbed my hair and dragged me upstairs and told me that when he said to come to bed, he meant right now.

"Daytimes, he would go to a construction job across town. I hurried to do the housecleaning and cooking quickly so that I could rest for a half hour or so before he got home. I had to tell him when I was going shopping for groceries. He wanted to know my every move all the time. I liked to talk with my neighbor, Macy. We didn't talk about anything very important, but it was nice to have someone to call a friend. He found me in her yard when he came home early one afternoon and ordered me to get into the house at once. I was embarrassed, and when I got inside I asked him why he did that. He called Macy a gossiping bitch and told me never to talk with her again. The only way I could manage a few minutes of talking with her was to go out back and work in the garden when she was working in hers.

"Another time he saw the meter reader coming from the back of the house where the electric meter was. I have never seen a man become so angry in my life. He insisted I was secretly seeing the man, and he hit me when I told him I was not seeing him. He called me a lying bitch. That was when I realized two things. He was drinking liquor each day in greater quantities even before he got home, and I didn't even like him. I don't know if I did not smell the liquor on his breath before or if I had smelled it and just let it pass without realizing what was causing his violent behavior.

"Still, whenever we went to church and when he was working daytimes, or doing his civic duty as a Boy Scout leader, he appeared to be a gentleman. I could not understand why he was so cruel to me. Everyone had told me he was such a good man. They still told me that as we left church after he had read Scripture for the congregation or sung a solo. He had a good, strong voice. Who would possibly believe me if I said that he was a cruel, wife- beating husband? Absolutely nobody, and I knew it only too well.

"A year went by, and I became more and more unhappy. I was crying a lot, but mostly when he was gone. I couldn't go back home to my parents. They wouldn't understand, and they would tell me I wasn't trying hard enough to be a good wife. They would say I needed to try harder, and not irritate him. So I had to live with my husband. I had to obey. After a while I learned when I could safely talk with him, and we did have moments that we even shared a laugh. Those times were usually when he had only two drinks in the evening. But after more than three, he became ill tempered. As time went on, the pattern of night time drunkenness became worse.

"He sometimes drank an entire bottle of liquor in the evening. Then he would keep me awake for hours listening to his ravings about something that had happened to him years ago, and how badly he had been used. If I yawned or said it was time for bed, he might throw a drink in my face. Once he even forced some of the foul stuff down my throat. Then he yanked me around, pulled my hair. I always thought he liked to hear me cry or scream out in pain, and he would bite me if he couldn't get a cry out of me otherwise. He was like the mad man in Dr. Jekyll and Mr. Hyde."

Astrid's eyes began to close. It was past midnight, time to sleep. She set the notebook aside on the night stand, feeling that she had been reading something that was not fiction but too awful to contemplate. The style was that of a diary, and now she believed that it was just that, Mrs. Guilford's diary, but probably written several years after the events.

"The poor woman. I'd have killed the pervert. Wonder what she did?"

ELEVEN
THURSDAY, AUGUST 31, 1989

Jason Trump slept the first two days after arriving home, worn out after the long hours of travel from Korea. No matter that his bed was unmade, he ignored the musty smell of a sheet that he took from the linen closet, used a pillow without a casing, and flung himself on the mattress to sleep. He couldn't remember ever feeling this tired in his life.

He woke up this mid-afternoon, rested and hungry. There was no fresh food in the house, but he recalled that his mother always said she wanted to be prepared with a supply of food in case of famine or severe weather. After searching through the kitchen cabinets, he went to the cellar door, which opened onto a wide platform with shelves on each side. This was her pantry.

"Bless her hoarding heart," he said when he found the shelves loaded with canned goods. He found sardines and a tin of unopened crackers, enough to satisfy his appetite until he could go shopping at the Spring Street Corner Grocery, three blocks away. At least he presumed it would still be open and operated by someone in the Underwood family.

When he finished his snack, he returned upstairs, all the way to the attic. His parents had not made a lot of changes in the house since he was a boy. What he hoped mostly was that they hadn't done away with his telescope.

And they had not. There it was by the window where he used to sit for hours, looking at everything around him...stars at night, neighbors by day. The attic had a dry, woodsy atmosphere, its unfinished open space providing the feel of an open rustic cabin, and Jason liked that. As a boy he played up here by himself, pretending he was a general in a great battle against Indians, always coming out the victor, single-handedly conquering a dozen red skins. He gave the conquered a taste of their own cruel methods and raised his knife in a gesture of victory.

Adult life was better. Each victory over a target brought a real reward--cash.

As an older man, he still felt the thrill of victory when he killed. He had no difficulty turning the target into his enemy, and the person who hired him could just as easily be the enemy. He sometimes thought he was a born killer. He eased into an adult criminal life because he had an appetite for it. And it all started right here, in the cozy attic where trunks provided old clothes, and an old pistol for make-believe. The knife was a sharp butcher knife that he hid under the eaves. His mother searched all over the kitchen for it, but ended up buying a new one.

Remembering the knife, Jason went to the rear of the attic and knelt down to feel along the eave on the left side. Yes! He brought out the butcher knife, ran a finger along its sharp edge, and grinned.

"I'm in business."

This was home. And now he had to consider the job ahead. Doris Guilford must have received his letter by now. He posted it four days ago at Logan Airport. Blackmail was a new game for him, but if he picked it up as easily as he did all the other tricks of his trade, be should have no difficulty relieving Doris of some of that money her husband hid at home.

It was here that he learned so much about the Guilfords. Their house, straight across the back lot, gave him an unobstructed view of everything that happened behind the house. Sometimes, Frank Guilford left the tool shed door open, and through his telescope, Jason could see what Frank was doing. He worked some with wood, but when he wasn't working on an outside job, just before supper, he would sit in a chair, drinking. He kept a cow bell beside him, and when his glass was empty, he'd ring the bell for Doris to come out with a fresh drink, and she exchanged that for the empty glass. He had to be admired for having her so well trained.

Jason hadn't been so successful in training his wife because Mi Hi's mother and father lived with them. But, to be honest, he preferred loving her to bullying her. He was disappointed when they had no children, and he knew it had to be her fault, just like the Eye was her fault. She did things to punish him because she didn't like his work. Well, he brought in a lot of money doing what he did. If he killed someone, he was paid well for the effort. And robberies brought in even more money. She liked that just fine.

He was here now, and that life in South Korea didn't

matter. The important thing from now on was to get money.

Among the things he learned about the Guilfords was that Doris was frightened of her husband. One late evening, Jason saw her run out of their kitchen door and into the back yard with him after her, yelling obscenities. If other neighbors saw or heard those things, no one said so.

Jason always thought Mrs. Guilford must be a witch to live with, since Frank was kind and helpful to the youth in his Boy Scout troop, and he had a reputation for being a man of principle. Even when he was chasing and yelling at her, Frank looked drunk, not harmful. Anyway, out in the yard he didn't touch her.

Doris Guilford worked after Frank died. Jason couldn't remember just what she did, but one of his mother's letters told him that. Seemed like she might have worked in the bakery.

No doubt Doris would not want anyone to know what Jason knew about her. She deserved to be blackmailed, as far as he was concerned, and she could pay up. He knew that for certain. Frank Guilford had not been secretive about the money he made on the Sears houses. He also boasted that he didn't trust banks, so he hid his money at home. Jason had a pretty good idea where that was.

If the damned war hadn't started up, this could have been done all those years ago. He'd have been a rich man then, but it wasn't too late now. Maybe it was even better now. When he was young, he would have squandered the money on booze and babes. Now, those interests were less important to him than just having status in this town, like Frank did. His own father had no spine, not like Frank. He wanted to be what Frank was—a respected citizen. After all, Frank was more or less his role model as he was growing up. Jason determined that he, too, would gain respect and would volunteer just enough so that he'd gain a strong foothold in the community. After a life of anonymity in a foreign country, it was time to become a gentleman. And then? Well, who knew? Maybe he'd court a rich older woman and gain a fortune before he checked out of this life.

He pulled the telescope up at the window and fixed it so that he could see the back of the Guilford house. Nothing had changed. From what he saw coming in from the airport, Fairchance hadn't changed all that much, either, except that it looked prettier now. Even the downtown shops were mostly the same. In the taxi, as he rode home down Main Street, Jason mentally named each shop as if it were yesterday that he left: the Five and Dime, furniture store, the book and stationery shop, hardware, bakery, Coty's Drugs, shoe stores, the State package store where he finally got to buy his first bottle of whiskey, Ruben's Jewelry, the banks, real estate and insurance companies. Most had a new owner's name, but basically they were the same businesses, refreshed by paint and awnings. The one change he noticed, in particular, was the Mid-Town Diner, which was being re-built. He remembered that his mother wrote about a fire and a murder. Jason didn't know that man.

The back yard between his house and the Guilford lot

had been mowed recently, judging by layers of dried grass. Of particular interest was the pine tree, taller than his house. It wasn't there a few days ago. It must have grown up quickly, overnight almost.

"Yes," he muttered, "I'm right back where I was only a few nights ago. Thinking the same thoughts. What the hell. I'm the same man, so why wouldn't I think the same? Never did change, and never will change. I've got to take care of myself. No one else will. Money is something I'll never pass up, and I don't give a damn how I get it."

He studied the area through his telescope until it was almost dark. Ready to call it a day and go back downstairs, he suddenly saw what he thought he'd never see again. The Eye.

"No, not you! How did you get here? You're supposed to be in Korea. Go back. I don't want to see you."

He stood back from the telescope. The Eye glared at him. It looked bigger than it did before. Where did it come from? This was Fairchance. This was home, not that dream in South Korea. Jason knew he hadn't really been there, only dreamed it. He'd never left home.

Running downstairs to his bedroom, he shut the door and dropped face-down on the bed. Pulling the pillow over his head, he screamed, "Go Away!"

After several minutes, he pushed the pillow away and sat on the edge of the bed, looked around, peeked upward, saw no Eye.

"There. I knew it was all a dream. Just a dream. I've never left here. I'm safe. And I'll go see Doris Guilford and she'll invite me in for coffee and cookies and I'll tell her that I dreamed I was in another country for many years and I'll tell her that I saw her last night and she'll cry and say okay what do you want and I'll tell her I want that money that Frank hid and she'll give it to me so I won't tell and we'll be friends. We'll always be friends."

TWELVE
FRIDAY, SEPTEMBER 1, 1989

Astrid smelled the coffee before she got all the way downstairs. Since Abram was the only other person in the house, he must have made it, but she found it hard to believe that he could make coffee, or do anything else, so soon. She never realized how badly a shoulder injury could debilitate a person until she observed his grimaces whenever he moved. Even sitting still without movement, his body language told her he had all he could do not to moan.

"Good morning," he said when she entered the kitchen. "I couldn't seem to manage pancakes, but there's toast and coffee ready for you."

"Mornin'. Godalmighty, Abram, you're doing too much. How'd you ever make coffee?"

She sat down and smiled as he poured a cup for her.

"Thanks," she said. "You're just too much. You have a bad night?"

"Oh yes. And how about you? Busy day ahead?"

"Busy, as always. I'll wash your back before I go, and help you into a clean shirt."

"Yes, mother."

"If I were your mother, I'd help you with the rest."

"Don't you worry about the rest. I can manage."

Astrid laughed.

"Don't look so serious. I was kidding. Before I forget to ask, did you happen to hear the noises last night? I keep hearing something out by the tool shed. I was going to come down, but I didn't want to wake you up. You didn't hear anything?"

"No. What did it sound like?"

Astrid watched his clumsy attempts at buttering his toast with the knife in his left hand while he held the bread to the plate with the fingers protruding from the right arm sling.

"You want some help there, son?"

"Very funny. No. I can do it. So, what sounds did you hear?"

"I'll get the jam." She went to the cupboard and brought out a jar of strawberry jam. "I'm not sure what the sounds were, to tell the truth. Some banging and jangling. At first I thought someone was out there, but the more I listened, the more I thought it might be an animal."

"I can check and see if anything has been taken or moved, or if there are animal signs. Could be a racoon."

"Could be. Or a cat or dog. Tonight I'll come down if I hear it again."

"You won't check it out alone. I'll go with you. If it's a prowler..."

"Prowler. Damned nonsense. Why would anyone prowl around this old house? If it stood empty for nine years without being broken into, nobody's going to prowl around here now when someone's living here."

She unscrewed the jam jar cover and spread a thick layer on her toast, all the while knowing full well that she had entertained that same idea last night. She remembered that the first night she spent in the house, when she was alone, she heard sounds. She finally convinced herself that nothing was amiss, and even laughed that there was no such thing as a haunted house. But, she wouldn't admit to Abram how the thought of a prowler crossed her mind more than once. He was alone here during the daytime. It wouldn't be right to express fear that someone might break in on him, not in his condition.

"Want some?" she asked, holding the knife in the air.

Abram's longing look said yes even though he said no.

"Oh, just stop it." She took his plate and slathered jam on his toast.

"There. Now, today the roofer is due to come and fix those leaks, you remember. At least we can get that done now before it rains. They're predicting rain next week."

"I remember, and I'll take care of it."

"Also, that toilet upstairs flushes every so often. You know what causes that?"

"It needs a new flapper. You can pick one up at the hardware store, and between the two of us, we'll install it. I won't be able to manage it, but I can tell you how."

"A flapper? Okay. That's good. I'll do that. I'd like to learn home repairs that I can do myself."

She saw that she'd said the right thing. He had a way of pursing his lips to the side and looking down when he was secretly amused or pleased about something. Of late, her plan to please and not offend had been working out. It shouldn't surprise her, but sometimes, like now, seeing a favorable reaction to her words did remind her that being nice paid off. But being bold still worked, too, recalling the hearing and how the entire room went silent when she got up to speak. Then, to have Natalie's praise--well, it was almost too much.

"Did you order the newspaper subscription?" Abram asked, breaking into her thoughts.

"Yes. Yesterday at the office. I called and they said they'd start it tomorrow morning. I called too late for it to be delivered today."

"Good. I miss a morning paper."

They finished breakfast, and Astrid helped Abram by bathing his upper body and assisting him into a clean shirt, then she cleaned up the kitchen, all before heading for the door to go to work.

"Busy day today, so I'll see you about five-thirty," she said. "Read some more of the diary."

"That what you think it is, a diary?"

"Looks like it to me. See what you think as you go on."

Driving to work, she let her thoughts return to that poor woman, married to a monster whom everyone called a good man.

"How can anyone be so callous, so lacking in compassion for others? Well, as the Shadow used to say, 'Who knows what evil lurks in the hearts of men? The Shadow knows.'"

At the memory of the old radio program, Astrid laughed like the announcer did, but the thought of evil lurking in the hearts of people was agonizing. Even her own occasional angry outburst could make her feel rotten afterward if she hurt someone's feelings. But to inflict pain simply for the enjoyment of it was horrifying. Did evil-doers regret their actions or have any conscience at all? She had read that some killers had hallucinations, and some heard voices telling them to kill so that they would be relieved of their own inner pain. Others, the article said, derived sexual pleasure from murdering, and still others killed because they hated their mothers. The list of causes for deviant behavior went on and on. Not only that, murderous behavior was not peculiar to one gender, though men were more often the offenders.

Why humans lacked compassion would forever mystify her. To think that there were men in society like Ted Bundy who would have kept on killing if he hadn't been caught. She read about his horrific murders and acts of necrophilia. The media reported that he had killed at least twenty young women, likely more. When he was finally executed in January, Astrid reassessed her previous strong argument against capital punishment, now convinced that the only way for society to react to that kind of inhumanity was to do away with it. As far as she was concerned, the world was better off without Bundy, and Florida's electric chair was more humane than he deserved.

"We can't let people do horrible things to others and then be so kind as to feed, clothe, and give them a comfortable living in the name of human decency and forgiveness as if the lives of the ones they murdered so inhumanely aren't important. We have to take a stance, make a judgment, and mete out punishment to fit the offense, even if it is Old Testament teaching."

She realized that she was shouting the words and waving her hand to emphasize her argument as she stopped her Jeep in the parking lot. Looking around to see if anyone noticed, she gathered up her things and opened the door to exit.

"Good morning, Astrid."

Oh no. It was Mr. Cornell, the publisher. She hadn't seen him, but he must have seen her animated discussion with herself. If only she could make herself invisible.

"Good morning, Mr. Cornell. Helluva nice day, huh?"

"That it is," he said.

His smile looked just a bit broader than it should for passing the time of day, Astrid thought.

THIRTEEN

Natalie and Dee were already at their desks when Astrid arrived, each typing up notes. Sometime during the night the air had changed, and now it felt cold and clammy in the office.

"You two got an early start."

Astrid rubbed her hands together to warm up and wring out some of her tension, while she looked at the clock to see if she was late. Three minutes to eight was not too late.

"We have a lot to do before next week's Zoning Board hearing," Natalie said. "And there's been a drug bust at the college."

"Ya? I thought it was a drug-free school."

"Is there such a thing today?" Dee said. "Used to be a few college kids would get drunk and cause a disturbance, maybe spend a night in jail. But today it's all about drugs and overdosing, lives ruined forever. What a shame things have changed so."

"Seems that Orientation got out of hand in one of the dorms," Natalie said.

She was all serious, one of those days when she barely heard what was going on around her. Already Astrid knew when to wait and listen, then act without comment. For two lovely ladies, Natalie and Dee could make one nervous with their intensity sometimes. And, for certain, the clothes they wore didn't come from the consignment shop, like most of Astrid's did.

"Dee, you have more experience with drug-type problems than either of us," Natalie said, "so you can see Police Chief Nolan to get details on their raid--how many students involved, where they are now, what are the charges they face, and what punishment the law will administer. Then go to the college and ask to see the P.R. director. Her name is Andrea Baker. All college news of this sort must go through her. But, if you get a chance to sneak down the hall, you may be able to step into President Dennis Mahoney's office and ask a few questions. He's quite genial, and sometimes offers a comment or two. Do it after Andrea has had a chance to give you the official notice. You may be able to get a good quote from him on what the college plans to do about discouraging drugs and alcohol on campus."

"Okay. I'll dig around a bit and see if I can find out if this is a one-time thing, or if they've had other incidents that haven't been reported. You want pictures with this?" Dee asked.

"Take a photo of the dorm where the raid occurred. Other students may not be happy about advertising it, but they'll just have to learn that life isn't always fair. Screw up and you pay, just like everyone else. Too many think they can get away with any behavior, break the rules, and that they shouldn't be punished. Well, it just doesn't work that way."

That Natalie came down so hard on college students

who were likely just experimenting baffled Astrid. The outrage seemed almost personal. Not like her at all.

"Astrid, that leaves the other assignment to you. I want you to dig around and find out whether Randall King made the contact with Construcorp to interest them in coming to Fairchance. Or is it possible that the contractors approached him about their desire to bring a shopping center here, and, if so, when did they do that? My suspicion is that King went to Mrs. Wolf about buying her farm after he knew that the company would pay a high price for a property they could use. Perhaps you should start with her. Ask if she had intended to sell before King approached her. She has nothing to hide now, if they have closed on the sale."

"Ya. They did that. He has a free and clear title to it."

"Good. Find out if she's still in the area. Then it shouldn't be too difficult to get that information. In the meantime, I'll..."

Her phone buzzed, and Natalie picked up the receiver.

"Mrs. Burke. May I help you?" she said.

Her eyes quickly focused on the desk. As the caller talked, she turned her chair toward the Main Street window. She placed her elbow on the desk and pressed her fingers against her left temple.

"So what do you think we should do?" she asked, in a hushed tone.

Finally, she heaved a big sigh and said, "Okay. We'll have to talk about it tonight," and hung up, still facing the street. She was slow in turning around and facing the other two.

"That was Drew. Our older daughter, Sally, kicked her sister in the leg this morning. Drew says she has a hairline fracture."

Natalie shook her head, desperation misting her eyes.

"Sally has always been too aggressive, but lately she's started to show this vicious side that is so terribly frustrating. This is the worst that she's done. Obviously, we've got to discipline her. Drew thinks we should confine her to her room for three or four days. I'm not so sure that it would do any good. She has too many things to keep herself amused there. Probably we need to get professional advice about this behavior."

She waved her hand in the air, dismissively.

"Well, we'll figure it out. In the meantime, as I was saying, I'll make some phone calls here to find out what I can about this Construcorp, things we don't already know. It appears that the company is reputable, but who knows for sure? The two attorneys at the hearing didn't say anything, as I expected they would."

"They were lawyers?" Astrid said.

"Yes. I heard that from the Fairchance lawyer sitting next to me in the front row. So let's go. We need to burn shoe leather on this one."

* * *

Getting out of the office was always one of the perks for Astrid in working as a reporter. But this assignment was far from a free day in the outdoors. For one thing, she feared that Natalie might be feeling a great deal of stress. That could be her daughter's problem, too. Sally's mother was at her job more than she was home these days. Undoubtedly Drew spent a great deal of time at the hospital. Absence of parents could mean Sally wanted attention, maybe even resented her younger sister for getting more than her share of notice. Even though it wasn't her problem, Astrid worried about the family.

Before leaving the office, Astrid had made a telephone call to the listed number for Mrs. Wolf and, in talking with her, learned that she was given two months to find another place to stay and, yes, she said she'd be glad to see Astrid. It seemed a pity that an old woman had to move from her long-time home. Recalling her own grandfather's objection to being taken to the hospital, Astrid wondered why some family member didn't move in with Mrs. Wolf and care for her in return for the title to the farm when she died.

It was a lovely day under a cloudless sky. The brisk air was so clarified that Astrid felt as if she could stand on top of Mt. Katahdin and see all the way to China, like they used to say when she was a child. She had a sudden yearning to be back on the farm herself. Rural living gave her a feeling of freedom that just wasn't the same as city life. Had she not wanted to live within a short distance of her work place, she would have considered being a couple of miles out of town. Still, she didn't regret the house she bought. When Abram was healed enough to work, the place would take on a whole new personality. It would never be a showplace, just a pretty, upgraded home.

Following instructions, Astrid had now arrived at the edge of a birch grove, a stately stand of white trees, mottled with black spots and strips of peeling bark. Beyond the trees, a lush green carpet of field spread along the road, and in the center of the field stood a large white Victorian house, not the typical Maine country home, but the type usually found in classy city neighborhoods where money was no object in creating unique effects like decorative filigree atop the wrap-around porch, lead glass windows, even a turret with arched windows. The white barn had similar character, with royal blue window awnings along the front. It looked like another house. The paved drive started at the road and widened to cover a large parking lot between house and barn.

"They'll tear it all down," Astrid said aloud, feeling agony over the callousness of the proposition.

She could envision this and the white birches all gone, replaced by a gaudy shopping center, with Ferris wheel entrance and the fetching sign Wonderland, and the thought made her angrier.

She turned the Jeep onto the driveway and looked from side to side, more and more upset that this beautiful land and its distant woodlands could all be gone in a few short months if Construcorp wasn't stopped. If ever she felt that she was part of an important cause and that the newspaper had a duty to inform the public, it was now. She had never believed the paper was much more than an opportunity to display her writing talent until this proposed atrocity to a beautiful setting, outstanding buildings, and a pure way of life. She had not experienced a tornado, but had heard that its approach sounded like a locomotive. That was happening here. A tornado, like a high-speed train, would sweep through in such a devastating manner that people would suddenly wake up and ask how it had happened… *if* the project was approved.

"It mustn't be."

She parked in front of the barn and walked to the porch, where she knocked at the side door. Wearing a pair of new slim jeans and a bright yellow polo shirt, the woman who answered resembled no old woman that Astrid ever knew. She was maybe five-four, without a trace of gray in her permed auburn hair. High cheekbones added to her youthful appearance. She could pass for forty.

"Miss Thorpe?" Mrs. Wolf said. "Come in. You called just as I was coming through the door. Been to the hairdresser's. I always hate a new perm, don't you? Oh, but you don't perm your hair, do you? You don't know how lucky you are. Mine is like baling wire. Can't do a thing with it. Come to the dining room. We'll sit at the table and talk. Coffee?"

"No thanks. You are Mrs. Wolf, I take it."

"My goodness, what a wonderful voice you have. Yes, but call me Chris. Lost my husband this year, and it's been hard to keep up with all the work. Now I have only a couple of hired hands, but we used to have four. Well, you know how it is. Help these days keep one eye on what they're doing and the other eye on the clock. Some days I don't get done in the barn until nine o'clock. But I have found a buyer for the herd, and they'll be gone on Monday."

Astrid took a deep breath in empathy for Chris Wolf, who seemed never to breathe between sentences.

"You don't have family, Chris?"

"No. The good Lord didn't bless us with children, and I was an only child. So was Oliver. And our parents died long ago. When Oliver died, I was left all alone with only the animals and farm workers to keep me company. I do have a cat and a dog, and they're my children. But, thank God, I'm fit as a fiddle. Lots of life in me yet. But I must tell you. I was relieved when Mr. King said he wanted to buy the farm. I've had quite enough of farming. I think I'll go to Florida and see what that's all about. They say it's sunshine all year round and that retirement communities offer a whole lot of activity for people. Who knows? I might even find a new man. Ha…I guess I should say an old man. At my age, that's about all I can hope for. I'm not looking, mind you. But one should never close doors or eyes."

Astrid couldn't hide a smile. If it weren't impolite to do so, she'd love to ask Chris her age.

"Well, Chris, I'm here to ask a couple of questions about the sale of your property. You do know what Mr. King wants to do with it, don't you?"

"I do now. He didn't tell me that he planned to resell the place when he came out and all of a sudden up and offered to buy it. But I read in your paper about the shopping mall. Well, it's his now, and he can do what he wants to with it."

"You have somewhere around ninety acres, don't you?"

"I had a few more than that, yes. We owned all of this farm and the next one up the road. It's where our farm manager, Felix Fenway, and his family live."

"And didn't Mr. King buy both places?"

"That's right. He asked for one deed to both places, so I had it drawn up that way. Should have done that in the first place. We should have added the other farm to the deed with this one, but my husband said we might want to sell that one sometime in the future, so the deeds were separate."

"And it doesn't upset you that they'd destroy all the buildings, trees, fields, and put in a concrete runway of stores and parking lots over both farms?"

"Upset me? Oh, I suppose I'd rather they didn't. But I was a city girl before I married Oliver. And when shopping centers came in, I took to them. I like to shop at malls. If the citizens of Fairchance want it, then it's okay by me. I won't be here to see it, anyway. And for the price he paid me, well, I can't complain."

"It's public record, but will you tell me what he paid you?"

"Oh sure. He paid me three hundred fifty thousand for it. Imagine. Oliver and I paid twenty thousand for this one and five thousand for the other one. Of course, land prices were a lot different in the forties."

She laughed and slapped her hand on the bare table top.

"I ask you. Prices soaring like that, where is this country going? But I shouldn't complain."

Astrid shook her head. More than anything, she wondered how the woman who lived here for forty years could give up such a lovely spread, and at that price. The house alone was worth more than that.

"Do you worry at all about what such a project does to the environment by replacing the good earth with concrete?" Astrid asked.

Maybe it was an impertinent question, but she thought people were altogether too oblivious to preservation these days.

"The environment? Don't tell me you're a tree-hugging Democrat. I feel this way, dear. I have some good years ahead of me, and as long as no one gets real foolish and drops an atomic bomb on us, I don't think I'll see this country dry up and blow away in my lifetime."

Astrid could have argued that Chris wasn't the center of the universe and that other generations of human beings might damned well like a chance to live comfortably, too, but decided she already risked being blamed as an insulting bitch and should just wrap it up before she stood a chance of losing a good position.

"Politics and environment aside," she said, "as I understand it, Mr. King didn't tell you about the possibility of a shopping center being built on this land. But did he give you any reason for his wanting to buy it? Did he say he wanted to live and farm here?"

"Actually he did. He said he wanted to bring his children up in fresh country air. I've known his wife since they moved here, more than I knew him. I gave knitting lessons in an evening crafts program at the high school, and she was a member of my class. I had no reason to doubt his word. He didn't say anything about farming. I just assumed that he meant to be a gentleman farmer. After all, this is a lovely place. The woods out back are beautiful, and we made trails for walking in summer and snowmobiling in winter. The house dates back to--well--I mean..."

Her voice faded away and she choked back the last words.

"You mean you really do not want to see it destroyed. Is that it, Mrs. Wolf?"

The woman got up and walked to the big bay window, framed by fresh white tiebacks. She stood at the center of the hand-braided rug covering nearly all the hardwood floor in the circular bay, turned and scanned the dining room, its hardwood door frames and antique furnishings, all polished, a sign of loving care. She gazed at the heirloom crystal in the china closet, the long mahogany table and six padded chairs with needlepoint covers, the large crystal chandeliere, the gold-framed antique mirror. She appeared to be seeing her work and life here for the first time. Maybe she was weighing the sacrifice she'd made for money in a different light. A rare, country house like this was worth more than any amount of money. It was a place that Astrid would love to own.

"I...don't...know what I was thinking. It isn't that

I didn't have enough savings to retire on. Oliver and I had saved. I could have sold the place for less and lived comfortably."

Then, as an afterthought, she said, "But I did think he meant to live here, you see. He did tell me that. I was very surprised when I read about the mall plans."

* * *

When she left the farm, Astrid went directly to Randall King's office. He lied to Chris Wolf, misrepresented his intentions, and led her to believe he'd keep the farmstead as it was. Whether or not she felt indifferent didn't matter, but Astrid had seen that Chris Wolf did care. It hurt her to think of its being destroyed. King should be held accountable for his actions, if no more than to be stopped and left with that farm on his hands. Obviously he could get his money back on a sale, but it would fall far short of what Construcorp would pay.

The more she thought about it, the angrier she became. She would give a lot to own a place like that farm. If King succeeded in creating a plaza over all of it, Fairchance would begin to lose its charm as a friendly, closely knit small city, and another working farm would be gone along with its rare set of buildings. Downtown shops would suffer and several would close. Everyone knew it.

But what if the public suddenly decided it wasn't such a bad idea, and let the Zoning Board go ahead with granting a variance for the sake of new jobs and the novelty of a shopping center at their back door?

"Dammit. We can't let that happen."

FOURTEEN

She seldom felt tired, but when she arrived home after work, Astrid could not face an evening of scraping and sanding woodwork as she had planned to do. The interview with Chris Wolf had stirred so much inner conflict that she was drained of all energy by the time she had the story written at her desk. It wasn't just her disgust at the callousness shown in the deal of the farm property that wore at her, but she was also disturbed by the obvious agony that Natalie was quietly going through. She tried to hide it, but the very air felt heavy around Astrid and Dee. From time to time they looked at each other in understanding, saying nothing while Natalie withdrew deeper into her thoughts, sharing no more of her worry with them.

"Hi, I'm home," Astrid called out as soon as she opened her own front door.

"Hey. I'm in the kitchen."

Astrid set her pocketbook on the hall table at the foot of the stairs and went into the kitchen where she found Abram at the table with the diary in front of him.

"I see you've been reading about the marriage of the century," she said on her way to the pantry to find something she could heat quickly.

"It's the ugliest one of the century, all right," Abram said. "Gets worse and worse."

"Ya? Do you feel like reading some to me while I heat something up for supper? You want macaroni and beef with meat sauce?"

"Sounds good."

His half-shut eyes and hard breathing told Astrid that he was struggling to be up and about. One thing for sure, she thought, he was determined.

"I'll just tell you what I read today," he said. "We can go on from there later on."

"Ya, fine. You like coleslaw?"

"Sure. Well, today I read about the old man's increasing problem with alcohol. The funny thing about it was that he didn't go anywhere when he was drunk. Just stayed home and made his wife's life a living hell. She tells about the time he came home late, and she had baked salmon and taken it out of the oven, expecting him to sit down to eat. But by the time he was ready to eat, the supper was cold, and he went wild. Mind you, he only had one drink at the time, as far as she knew. She wrote that it was fall, and beginning to get quite cold outside. He started to rip at her clothes. I wonder why he did that. He always seemed to be ripping her clothes. She wanted to save some of her dress from being torn, so she ran out the back door, and he right after her with a cleaver in his hand."

"My God. She should have called the police. Or someone in the neighborhood should have."

"I guess they didn't do that so readily back then. It was the mid-forties, remember. People thought they should stay out of other families' domestic problems. Come to think of it, not much different today. No one wants to get involved."

"I guess so, but the neighbors must have seen some of these things. Someone should have helped her. What did she do?"

"She said there wasn't any place to go, so she backtracked to the house and ran up the stairs. He wasn't as agile as she was, so by the time he got to the bedroom, she had taken off all her clothes and stood naked in the middle of the room. She knew he'd want to mount her on the bed, and that's what he did. You know, I'll bet that woman never once had a good sexual experience with her husband."

Astrid looked over at Abram, suddenly feeling warm. He had a look in his eyes that she interpreted as sexy, but which could simply be that he was reflecting on the suffering that the woman went through, or maybe his own pain gave him that distant look. For herself, Astrid wondered how good a sexual experience might be with Abram. She stood so long, holding the wooden spoon in her hand, that of a sudden, Abram shouted.

"Hey, somethin's burning."

"Oh damn. The macaroni is burned on."

"Never mind. Just scrape the good ones off and put them in another pan. You'll have a mess to clean up, but soak it overnight in baking soda and water, and it may not be too bad. Sure does stink, though."

She went back to putting the macaroni meal together. Seemed like he knew a whole lot more about food preparation than she did. Good thing. She was a disaster in the kitchen.

"Any more than that?" she asked.

"Oh, she goes on about her own feelings. She said she hated her husband more and more each month, but the months and years dragged on. She had no friends, and that's odd, too. As careful as he was not to be seen drunk outside his house, nobody ever came to call, and the only telephone conversation she ever had was with her mother. Once when the mother called, her husband answered and became abusive, called her a dumb witch, and told her she could write letters instead of tying up his telephone. That pretty much ended the mother and daughter contact. The man was a piece of work."

"A piece of rotten garbage, you mean," Astrid said.

"His ramblings were almost incoherent, she wrote, but one thing was certain. He was paranoid to the point of trusting no one. And that grew worse and worse. The nightly ramblings wore her down. In one place she wrote that she feared she was going as mad as he was."

"She needed help, that's for damned sure. Well, I guess the food is ready," Astrid said.

She dished it all up and sat down opposite Abram.

"Did you have a hard day?" he asked.

"I've had better. The phones never stopped ringing. Kept us busy answering all kinds of questions about the new shopping center, as if it was a sure thing. A few callers were ready to kill the Zoning Board members. I went to see Chris Wolf. She's the former owner of the farm site."

"She give you anything useful?"

"Oh ya. She seemed real happy that she got so much money, and at first didn't care that a shopping center might go in after tearing down her house and stripping the woodlands down to bare earth. But, as we talked and she began to think about how nice everything is, she looked like she wanted to cry and said maybe she made a mistake."

"Kinda late to think of that."

"As she damned well knows. But, the interesting thing is that King told her he was going to move his family out to live there. Now, that's a long way from the truth."

"Did he already have Construcorp in his pocket?"

"Well, then I went to his office, and after a lot of sidestepping, he finally said a Construcorp representative was at a conference he attended, and that the two of them started talking. He learned that the company was planning to expand its outreach and put a mall in Maine. King said he knew Mrs. Wolf wanted to sell out, and he tried to make light of all that transaction, but in the end, of course, it boils down to the fact that he secured the land first and then let the company know that Fairchance had an ideal site for a shopping mall."

"So he made an offer to Mrs. Wolf that he knew he could at least double in a sale to the company."

"And when our paper hits the street next week, everyone will know that. The whole thing stinks from beginning to end. I just hope people don't give up and say let them come in. I heard people talking after the hearing, and some of them who had raised their hands showing opposition to the project were already having second thoughts because the company's president, Mr. Carney, promised that many jobs would be created for the area. And, of course, our brilliant interim mayor spoke for the project, too, with the same promise."

Abram said nothing, and Astrid knew he was thinking of the jobs. He would like a chance to earn big money that the construction job would pay. Her wages were low for him by comparison, and other work just wasn't forthcoming.

They ate the rest of their meal in silence. He didn't eat much, and Astrid understood. Painkillers lessened appetite. The fact that he had come to the kitchen and carried on as he did surprised her.

"You can't be feeling very good yet," she said. "You up for ice cream?"

"Sure. I don't refuse ice cream."

When she sat down again, he said, "I almost forgot to tell you. I found your prowler today behind the shed."

"You've been very active today. It surprises me. You aren't overdoing, are you, Abram?"

"Naw. I'm just fine when I'm full of pills. Besides, I've been sleeping a lot, too."

"So what about the prowler?"

"It's a cat. A young one, I'd say, since it's not very big. Pretty though--black with white markings. I left some milk in a dish for it. You want to keep it? Seems to be a stray."

"I like cats. We always had two or three on the farm. Let's take a look after supper, if it's still here."

"I'm sure it will be. Seemed to be settled in behind the small wood pile. Oh, and I had a visitor, too. This one *was* a person. He's a neighbor, across the back yard."

"Who?"

"His name's Jason Trump. He said he just returned from South Korea where he's lived ever since the war. He was one of those who married a native Korean and stayed on. His wife died, and he decided to come back and settle into his family home, now that his parents are gone, too. I'd say he must be about sixty. Not a big man, about five seven or so. Looks older because his hair is almost all white. He's a very strange guy. He never really looks at you when he talks, and sometimes he even turned his back on me. He said he saw me out there with the cat and thought he'd come over and introduce himself."

"That was nice of him. Haven't had any other neighbors come in yet."

Astrid started to wash the dishes while Abram told her about Jason Trump's visit.

"Well, I don't know how nice it was. He seemed very interested in Mrs. Guilford, wondered if she was still living here. Said they were good friends before he went to war in Korea. I told him I thought she was in a Bangor nursing home."

Abram fell quiet, watching Astrid work at the sink. She sensed that his eyes were on her every move and asked herself why he was being so attentive. She was never good at reading men, even though she lived mostly among men growing up. They always seemed to have a secret agenda, even when talking about serious things. Maybe that's why she had become loud and straightforward. It had a protective effect.

"Something else," Abram added. "Jason said he mailed

a letter to Mrs. Guilford and wondered if she had read it yet. I thought that a bit odd since I'd just told him she was in a nursing home."

"Did you tell him we have the letter?"

"Yes, and I came inside to get it. I took it out of the desk, and when I turned around, he was right at my back. Scared the shit out of me, to tell the truth. He just laughed, as if he'd pulled a real funny joke on me. To be honest, I don't take to him. If you're ever alone here, Astrid, and he comes to the door, don't invite him in."

"You think he's dangerous?"

"Could be. I'm all for giving a man a chance, but he strikes me as a little too weird. Later, he asked if I live here alone, and I told him I am staying with you until my shoulder's healed enough so I can do renovations on the house. His comment was, 'Good going. You're a man after my own heart. Take them rich and leave them poor, I always say.' If I'd had two good arms, I think I'd have challenged him on the spot. I did tell him he had it all wrong, not that it did any good. He just laughed again."

"Of all the nerve. Lucky I wasn't here. I'd have laced into him."

"No doubt. " He thought a moment before adding, "The really weird thing was when he left. He said 'Tell Doris I'll be over to see her when she's home.'"

"Wonder if he had shell shock in the war."

"Maybe. And maybe I got it all wrong. People make mistakes. Just seemed like a very odd slip of the tongue after I'd told him Mrs. Guilford was in a nursing home."

FIFTEEN

He was nearly caught. Jason had looked through his telescope to see what was going on this afternoon, but he saw no activity around the Guilford house. That's where he made his mistake. He hadn't seen anyone around the back shed since his return, and presumed that Doris Guilford didn't come outside often. At night he could see a light in her upstairs window, until midnight sometimes. But what Jason never expected was to see a man, with one arm in a sling, checking things out back.

He was already walking in that direction before he saw the man. Best way to handle it, he decided, was to go on and introduce himself. At the same time, he'd find out what was going on around there. Turned out that Abram Lincoln was a live-in with a woman named Astrid Thorpe, and she had bought the house from Doris Guilford. Now all he had to do was find Doris. He could still do the blackmail trick, no matter where she was. He knew she had money, and she would damned well pay him for keeping quiet.

But why settle for only that? He saw the state of the Guilford house when he followed Abram inside. He could offer to help with the renovation, and while at it, he could locate items of value, especially money. They must have credit cards and a checking account. He hadn't planned on returning to his sleight of hand tricks in removing money from accounts, but if opportunity was right at his doorstep, why not?

The more he thought about it, the more he liked it. All he had to do was introduce himself to the little lady who bought the house, since she must be the one with the money, and offer his free services as something to keep him busy until he found a permanent job. Women were such a pushover, he'd have no trouble at all. It was obvious that the handyman she was taking care of--and Jason was sure she was doing that okay--was nothing but a wimp. The tall ones always thought they were above the rest, literally, but they broke at the knees just like anyone else.

Things were shaping up.

"Now, where do you suppose Doris went? If I wait a few days, she'll come back to her house. I'm sure of that. She wouldn't just leave it and not come back. It's not like her to do that. She never goes anywhere, so of course she'll be back."

Then he remembered.

"Oh, she's in a nursing home in Bangor. I can find her. If she wants me to bring her home, I can do that."

* * *

The telephone rang so seldom that Astrid jumped when it buzzed. She threw the paint scraper to the floor and headed to the kitchen to answer.

"Who can that be?" she said as she passed Abram in his chair. He followed and stood by her when she answered.

"Hello."

She saw Abram wince, and realized that she had bellowed into someone's ear.

"Astrid."

She knew the voice. Her brother's voice didn't penetrate like hers, but it was healthy, also.

"Hi, Gunnar. This is a surprise. What's up?"

They seldom talked by phone, so she worried that one of his family might be seriously ill.

"I hear that you're trying to keep a shopping mall out of Fairchance. Right?"

"Right. It's turning into quite a battle."

"I wouldn't ask what side you're on, even if I didn't know."

His snort expressed his disdain for her stand against what she knew he would call progress.

"Ya. You can be sure of it. So what...?"

"I want to be at the next public hearing on the project. When will that be?"

"You? Why?"

"I have my reasons, Astrid. When is the meeting going to be?"

"It's next week. Wednesday at seven in the Court House. You have an interest in it, then?"

"Well, I figure this way. Knowing how dedicated to the cause you're bound to be, and that they may not settle there in Fairchance, I'm thinking my farm might be just the ticket for a mall."

"My God, Gunnar. A shopping center in Appleton?

You've got to be out of your mind. There can't be two thousand people around that whole area."

"No problem. People don't have to be next door to the mall. They'll drive twenty or thirty miles to get to one. You know that."

"They will, but usually that drive is a direct route on a main road. You're located on a side road, ten miles in. You want to sell out so badly? Why don't you just rent the farm to someone?"

"I don't want to rent it. There's got to be a way to take a profit out of all that land. Grampa should have left it to you, you love the land so much. You'd make a good farmer."

"Your memory is selective, Gunnar. You often told Grampa how you loved the place. He thought you'd be happy to have it and be self-employed. He made a lot of money from the farm products, and you can, too. But you've got to tend it. That north field, for instance. You really need to get onto that before it all goes back to woodland."

She was trying to sound sympathetic, but in fact was becoming frustrated with her sibling's laziness. She saw the farmland as an opportunity, and he saw it as a millstone around his neck. Why wouldn't he just roll up his sleeves and work the land? He had all the equipment made for upscale farming, including the biggest possible John Deere cab tractor with air conditioning, stereo, and everything but an Espresso machine.

"Thank you for your usual support, Astrid. I don't want to live like a slave to this farm and never be able to enjoy my money, like Grampa did. He didn't rest until he was on his death bed. I'll come to the meeting Wednesday. Maybe I can collar one of those big shots and interest him in coming to an area that won't give them so much opposition."

"Suit yourself. While I have you on the line, how's all the family? I haven't heard from anyone since I came here."

"Like you've been in touch with us, huh? Everyone's fine."

"And is Momma still planning to go to South Carolina? I should talk with her."

"She's not home right now. Gone to the movies. Ya, she says her sister can't be alone, so she's gong next month."

"The warmer climate should be good for her."

"Maybe. Well, I've got to go now. You come down and visit."

"I will, very soon. Love to everyone."

She hung up and found that Abram had gone back to his chair. While she loved her brother, this notion of becoming rich overnight by selling the farm was not new, and it infuriated her. He was like Mr. King, looking for a killing. She went to her chair next to Abram's.

"That your brother?"

"Ya."

"Sounds like you don't get along all that well with him."

"I do and I don't. He's a good enough man, but he has always resented that Grampa left me money and left him the farm. Actually, the farm is worth a whole lot, but he thinks the way it's worth a lot is to sell it for something like this shopping center project. Never mind that it's located in the boonies. I just don't understand his lack of reasoning. He keeps too few cows to make a profit in milk production, and he won't till enough of the land to amount to anything. He's letting good fields turn fallow. All he does is try to work out some scheme that will give him a lump sum fortune."

"From what I heard, he's going to try to sell to Construcorp?"

"Isn't that ridiculous? Well, let him try. Who knows. Maybe he'll surprise me and actually sell to them. I wish he would, though I hate to think of that farm being destroyed, any more than I can stand to see Chris Wolf's farm turned into a mall. Why can't things stay peaceful and nice? Why is someone always ready to upset things in life? And there are so few really good working farms now."

Abram leaned his head back. He must need another pain pill, Astrid thought. She noticed that his breathing was shaky.

"The answer to that is simple," he said. "Money. Profit's valued more than life, buildings, or beautiful countryside. It's the American way, don't you know. I predict the profit craze will eventually wipe out life as we know it. Profiteers never get enough. They reach too far and go too deep until they take that one final plunge for a bigger profit, and suddenly they find themselves with nothing left, drowning in debt."

"And how do you feel about it?" Astrid asked. "Are you satisfied to be poor?"

"Poor? I never thought of myself as poor. I work hard for every cent, and that's fine with me. Sure, I'd like to get onto a big construction job, but if I don't, I'm happy to renovate houses."

He gave her a wink and a smile.

"Lucky for me, then. And did the roofer come today?"

"Yup. We'll be dry for a while, until the house is moved and a new roof is put on. You do still plan to do that, right?"

"Yes, of course. Why do you ask?"

"Oh, just wondering. This interest you have in farmlands seems more than a looking-on but hands-off interest."

"You think I want to go into farming?"

"The thought did cross my mind."

"I'll admit I'm not like Gunnar. I do like working the land. I'm not too keen for livestock. But working in soil is very satisfying to me. And when I see corn stalks waving across acres of fields, it gives me a thrill. But, no. I'm not considering going into it. I love my job at *The Bugle*. I work with good people, and I like the outside assignments as well as writing and then reading my byline. It may be vain of me, but it's an exciting job."

"Uh huh."

"What. Is that supposed to mean something?"

"No. Just saying uh huh, that's all."

He tipped his head back again and closed his eyes.

But Astrid could see the wrinkling around his mouth. If he didn't have the bad shoulder, she'd go over and punch him. The idea of suggesting that she was a farmer at heart. Ridiculous.

"I'm going upstairs, Abram. I'm just too tired tonight to work on the woodwork or the toilet. I'll read the diary."

"Hey, I was thinking about that. If it's a diary, should we really be reading it? I mean, it's private stuff."

"Ya, it is. Maybe we shouldn't. Do you want to stop reading it now, before you find out how it all comes out?"

Abram scowled. Obviously Doris Guilford wrote about her own life, and it was just as obvious that she put up with her husband's abuse for years. But what happened? Did he abandon her in the end?

"I suppose since Mrs. Guilford left it in the house, where anyone could find it, that the new owner has a right to read it. If she had wanted it, or didn't want anyone to see it, she'd either have destroyed it or taken it with her. So, no. I don't want to stop reading it."

"Neither do I. That settles it."

"Wait. That settles it? You're not even going to contact Mrs. Guilford to find out if she wants the diary?"

"No."

Astrid went to the kitchen, picked up the notebook, and returned to the dining room.

"Here's a glass of water and a muffin to eat before you take a pain pill. You need anything else before I go up?"

"I'm okay."

"Goodnight then."

She knew he was watching her as she ascended the stairs to the landing, but she didn't look back. As far as she was concerned, anyone who left a private piece of work like a diary lying in plain sight in a house that was sold to a new owner had no interest in hiding anything. Astrid's honest opinion was that Doris Guilford wanted someone to understand what she'd been through.

If she wants a sympathetic ear, then she has it. I'm reading it through to the end. I don't care if it is her diary.

SIXTEEN

Settled in bed, Astrid adjusted the table lamp and opened the notebook resting against her raised knees. This was a cool night, but she had the window open as always and had a blanket over the sheet. It would be colder before morning.

A torn corner of the newspaper marked where Abram left off reading. No need to go over the previous material since he'd already told her all about it. Astrid read on and found that Mrs. Guilford digressed, explaining how she met her husband.

"Pa had gone to Fairchance with two other men to pay taxes, and to find the man who built Sears houses. One of the men had ordered a bungalow and needed help putting it up. Of course, they found Frank Guilford. So he was hired to come to Deergrove. That is the last town south in the county. In those days, people didn't have fast or very good cars, so he could not commute like people do today. He needed a place to live while the building was going on, and Pa invited him to stay at our house. That's how I met him."

Well, now Astrid knew for certain that this was a diary. Doris named her husband.

"He was always polite. He gave me no reason to think he was not the good man everyone said he was. He told me little things about his life, and I told him about mine.

The fact that he had his own business and could build houses impressed me. His looks were nothing outstanding. He was just an ordinary man with ordinary features.

"He had one more night to spend with us, and that evening he asked me to marry him. It was a surprise. I had little feeling for him, but after he returned to Fairchance, Pa and Mama kept telling me I should have accepted the offer. So when a letter came for me and it was another proposal, I wrote back that I would marry him.

"I have already written about our wedding day and the first night of our marriage. It should have been easier for me as time passed. Sometimes he showed a bit of compassion, but if he kissed me, it was hard and unfeeling. He looked at me with cold eyes. I never knew how he really felt about me, and I decided that I would ask him one evening before he had too much to drink."

Astrid's attention was drawn from the page to a sound out back. She listened until she heard it again.

"The cat. I should have fed him before I came up."

She got out of bed, donned slippers and robe, and tiptoed downstairs. Abram appeared to be asleep, snoring lightly with his head cocked to one side.

"Poor guy. Must be awfully uncomfortable," she thought.

She went to the kitchen and found leftover boneless chicken, cut it into small pieces and placed them on a plate. The back door squeaked when she opened it, and she stopped to hear if Abram stirred. Hearing nothing, she left the door open, not wanting to risk another squeak, stepped outside and looked all around.

"Here kitty," she called.

After calling a few times, she decided to leave the plate by the door. Just as she bent over, a movement by the tall pine tree caught her attention. That was no cat.

"Who's there?" she called.

No answer. She crouched down more and, in this position, backed slowly through the open doorway. She quickly turned off the light. Now whoever was out there most likely couldn't see her any better than she could see him. She waited and watched, still squat down low, and finally she saw another flash of white clothing going from the pine tree toward Spring Street. The thin slice of moon provided too little light to see who the man was, but he obviously had been close to her house.

She nearly fell over when Abram spoke behind her.

"What're you doing?" he asked.

Standing, Astrid closed the door and snapped on the overhead light.

"I came out to feed the cat," she said.

"Were you facing off with it?"

"Very funny. I saw a man running toward the pine tree and then he went on toward the street over there. It's Spring Street, I think."

"That's right. Did you see who it was?"

"It's too dark. I just saw that he was wearing white pants and shirt."

"Damn."

"What?"

"That Jason Trump was wearing all white when he came over today. What's he up to, I wonder."

"And I wonder if he's been snooping around here before. "

"I doubt it. He said he just got here."

"Well, tonight I thought it was the cat I heard, but there he was. And the cat didn't come when I called. I left some food for him."

"The cat?"

"No, the prowler. Of course the cat, you."

Astrid hoped this joking was a sign that Abram was feeling stronger, but knew in her heart that it would be a long while before he'd be ready to work much.

"There's something about him that I don't trust," Abram said.

"Jason?"

"No, the cat," Abram said over his shoulder on his way back to the dining room. Astrid followed.

"We'll just have to watch him, I guess," Astrid said. "And don't ask. I mean Jason. Are you warm enough? I'll get a blanket to put over you."

"Actually, I'm fine."

She was already up the stairs, and soon found a light blanket in a box that she hadn't unpacked yet. Back to Abram, she laid the blanket over him and tucked it in at the sides of the chair.

"There. It will be cold by morning. Now you won't freeze."

"Thanks. This nursing home provides good service."

Astrid hadn't meant to, but she placed her palm on Abram's cheek and looked into his eyes.

"It's in my interest to get you well."

She quickly pulled her hand away and ran up to her bedroom, with a feeling that he might have misinterpreted her touch. If he only knew. Her face had been so close to his. She pulled back just in time before giving him a kiss. Damn. Mustn't let that happen again. Whatever came over her? The funny part was that he looked like he would welcome a kiss.

Back in bed, she began to read again, but now she had distractions. Abram, noises out back, an unwelcome neighbor, as well as the intrusion of thoughts about the possible razing of that beautiful country home, all made it difficult to concentrate on the words. Finally, she closed the window and started to read where she began in the first place. She skimmed over what she remembered, and picked it up from there.

"Frank had developed a taste for manhattan. I'm not sure why the change, but I did notice that they acted more quickly than Scotch did. To top it off, he began to order me to mix his drinks for him, and though I hate the very smell of liquor, I fixed his drinks whenever he demanded.

"This one evening I handed him his third drink and took the chance of asking why he married me. I asked if he loved me at all. To my surprise, he set his drink down and told me to sit next to him. He said that at first he did not think much of me, but even though he acted crazy from drinking sometimes, he had grown to care for me. He admitted that sometimes when he woke up in the morning and saw a bruise on my face, he did not remember that he had hit me. That was all he said, and I didn't say any more. I suppose it was some consolation to know that he did not remember being brutal when he was too drunk. To get that much of a commitment from him was enough. So another year passed, and I tried to be more forgiving and to cooperate, even in bed. Maybe when I asked him if he loved me, he thought he should be gentler with me. Anyway, he was for a while, and that was fine for almost that whole year. Then he started being crazy again. It all started when he was fired from his job. I later learned that he was fired because he raced off the construction work and chased a woman down the street and did not return to the job for two hours, quite drunk. I have often wondered who she was, and if they knew each other years ago.

"This time it got harder and harder to forgive him for the harsh words and the backhand slaps across the face that he so often did. By the end of that year, I was beginning to wish I had never asked if he loved me. I was convinced that a man who loved a woman did not hit her and swear at her and call her cheap names.

"That winter I came down with pneumonia. Still I continued to cook and houseclean for Frank, and to mix his drinks. One day I passed out on the kitchen floor and Frank found me there when he came home. He got me to the hospital, and a doctor examined me. Of course he found the bruises. He asked me about them. I lied, though I should have told him that my husband beat me.

I felt that if I did that people might think I was to blame. They might say that if I did not nag him, he would have no reason to raise a hand to me. So I said I was accident prone and fell quite often. The doctor looked as if he knew I lied, but he could not do anything about it. It was my choice to keep my married life a secret.

"It was after I came home from the hospital that I began to think about how other women lived so happily with their husbands. I asked myself why our life could not be like that. And when I realized that I had married a man with two personalities and a thirst for liquor, then I thought of ways that I could leave him.

"But in all of my dreaming about freedom, I had no courage to do anything. I had no money of my own, no way to earn a living even if I could sneak enough cash out of his wallet to buy a bus ticket out of town. Each day I grew more depressed. What could I do? I had no friends to confide in. My father was sick with lung cancer, my mother never would understand or be able to help in any way. And there were no authorities I could go to, for everyone here knew Frank and believed that he was a good man. No one knew me well. I was stuck in this life of misery."

Astrid's eyes began to close. She yawned and set the notebook aside, snuggled down into the warm bedclothes, and tried to erase the picture of that pathetic woman from her mind before sleep overtook her.

SEVENTEEN
MONDAY, SEPTEMBER 4, 1989

For *The Bugle* editorial staff, Labor Day was no holiday. The newspaper had a deadline, and the three writers were dedicated to meeting it every week even when it meant losing a holiday. This week, the Zoning Board's decision on the proposed shopping center would have to share page one space with school openings and the college drug raid.

The weekend had gone too quickly for Astrid to accomplish all she had planned. The diary was forgotten both Saturday and Sunday. Not only did she scrape and varnish woodwork to a lighter shade, but she had long discussions with Abram on plans for the house renovations. He was eager to work, but she insisted he follow doctor's orders. On Tuesday he would see the orthopedic surgeon and soon begin physical therapy. Abram already had cabin fever. Sunday, Astrid had enough of his wandering about the house and fussing over things, so she ordered him into the Jeep and drove to the country, not by chance coming upon the Chris Wolf farm. She let the engine idle while they sat looking at the splendid white country home, the barn that looked like a house, and the various smaller buildings.

"This is Chris Wolf's property?" Abram asked. "I

thought a man by the name of Felix Fenway owned it. I did some repairs to the back porch after a bad storm hit and a tree branch broke through the roof. He was the one I dealt with. He paid me."

"Seems the Wolfs owned the farm up the road from this one. Fenway is the farm manager and lives at the other farm with his family. That farm was included in the sale, too."

"I didn't realize this was what you were talking about. You know that's some of the finest workmanship I've seen in any house. I guess I'd have to agree that destroying all that hand crafted work for a shopping center is almost sinful. Even if King has bought it, doesn't mean Construcorp can't be stopped. Why would anyone in their right mind want to ruin all this?"

"Money, I believe you told me." Astrid said. "I guess there's no room for sentiment when someone is determined to become a very rich person."

She felt easier now about opposing the mall, knowing that if it was not approved Abram wouldn't be angry with her for helping to rob him of a good job. And she didn't want him to be displeased with her.

The office was quiet, since the editorial room had the only workers in the building. It felt eerie to work in so much silence. The building ordinarily resounded with doors shutting and voices in the hallway, and when windows were open, the Main Street noises were constant.

Astrid noted that Dee had a deeper tan from her weekend in Twin Ports, where she had planned to visit with her friends and to work at The Lodge. Natalie, on the other hand, looked pale and drawn.

"Did you have a good weekend, Dee?" Astrid asked. "You got a lovely tan."

"I did. I sat out in a sunny sheltered corner and read a book. Stayed out almost too long, as you see. And I made notes about the book I want to write. I had dinner with my best friend and her family, and we watched a movie. And the weather was perfect. Yes, it was a great weekend."

"Sounds ideal." Astrid didn't hesitate to ask, "Do you have a male special friend there?"

"Astrid," Natalie said. "That's rather personal."

Dee laughed. "It's okay. No, I don't. I'm not sure if I'll take up with a man again. I had a very good husband. It's hard to think of replacing him."

"Ya. I guess it would be."

Astrid waited several minutes, knowing that she shouldn't be too personal as Natalie just pointed out, but her curiosity got the better of her.

"Did you get Sally straightened out, Natalie?" she asked.

Immediately, she wished she hadn't. As usual, the words were out before she weighed them carefully.

"Yes, I think we did, Astrid. Thanks for your concern."

Don't tell me I got it right this time, Astrid thought. Natalie always managed to surprise her.

"We told her she couldn't try out for the winter play at school unless she demonstrated that she could control her temper. She's a natural on stage and loves to perform, so I think the possibility that she might not be allowed to do that this year was more effective than as if we confined her to her room. I sat down with her and discussed her problem. At first she said nothing was bothering her, but then it slowly came out. She had the feeling that we were showing favoritism to June. I guess I thought she was more mature than she is and that she understood how we love both of them equally. But, children aren't a great deal different from adults. You have to keep reassuring them that you love them. Well, we hope we've begun to resolve the problem. They're both good girls."

She took off her reading glasses and closed her eyes, giving them a light massage.

"You seem very tired," Dee said. "Do you feel well?"

"It's been a strain. I thought girls would be so much easier to bring up than boys, but I have to tell you, the past couple of months have been a nightmare, trying to keep them from fighting, pouting, stomping around. I've lived in an insane asylum, I swear."

"Well," Dee said. "They'll grow out of it. Just be thankful that you have two healthy girls."

"Oh." Natalie put a hand to her lips and gave Dee a sympathetic look.

"I'm so sorry. I forgot about your loss. I really do know how fortunate I am. I guess I've been resenting Drew's extra hours at the hospital as much as anything else. He's tired, comes home and eats and goes to sleep in his chair. I don't know. Maybe we need a change."

She said the last very softly, as if she were thinking out loud. Astrid wondered what kind of change she was thinking of, but this time she managed to hold her tongue. That was likely a place she shouldn't go. If Natalie wanted to share thoughts of change, she'd tell them.

Since there was no mail delivery on this holiday, Natalie suggested they close up early after they had the week's issue basically complete.

"Do we have all of your drug raid story, Dee?"

"Yup. You may want to take a look at it. I'm just finishing the sidebar now. The students gave me as much as the PR director or the president did. They had some pretty strong sentiments against alcohol and drugs. I guess that surprised me, but they are very dedicated to issues that deal with environmental protection. They see drugs, in particular, as counter-productive to preservation. They were quite upset that a few students gave the college a bad name. I have to admire them."

"I'll read it before I leave today. And Astrid. Your story is ready to go, is it?"

"It is. Are you writing an editorial on Construcorp this week?"

"I have done that. So as far as I can see, we can mop up final details tomorrow morning."

* * *

Returning home, Astrid went to the dining room where she found Abram sitting peacefully with the black and white cat in his lap. The cat looked up, and blinked, its wide eyes expressionless, but it didn't jump away.

"That looks cozy," she said. The cat took off.

"You scared the kitty. I called the vet this morning, and

he said to bring her in Thursday afternoon. He'll spay her and do all the other stuff that needs to be done, shots and all."

"The vet was open for business today?"

"He said he's always open, just that the office door is closed. But anyone needing help will find him willing to open the door."

"So it's a she. How did you get her to come inside?"

"She was at the back door where you left the food, and I just took some more chicken and held it out so she could get a good smell, then I coaxed her inside with it. I think she must have had a good home before now, she's so well behaved. I called neighbors on this street and no one claimed her, so I guess she's ours."

"Then I guess she *is* ours," Astrid said.

That word *ours* seemed strangely correct, though this wasn't Abram's home, and she thought maybe she had taken in two strays.

"I'm going to change my clothes, and then paint the living room. I think it's ready now. You want to read to me while I work?"

"Read what?"

"The diary, of course. What else? I left off where the bookmark is."

Abram went to the kitchen and found the diary on the desk again, where Astrid had left it Saturday morning. When she came downstairs, he looked up from the table.

"I just caught up to where you left off. If you'll take the chair in, I'm ready to start reading there. We're almost finished with it, you know."

EIGHTEEN

"My frustration grew day by day until I thought I would take my own life," Abram read, as Astrid rolled white paint on a wall. "But I decided there must be a reason why Frank did what he did. I had to find out why he liked hurting me. It was not about love this time. I just wanted to know why. I handed him his drink after supper, and asked him why he hurt me so much and why he dwelt on the past so much. He said women make men feel small. He said they emasculate a man at his weakest moment and they laugh and say you are pitiful and not able to satisfy them. He said women deserve to be punished. That is what he told me.

"So I asked him how many women he was talking about. He said just one. And I said it was not me, so why did he punish me for something someone else did. His face grew dreadful dark and full of hate. I do not think he had ever looked quite so ready to kill me as right then. And I didn't care. I thought if he killed me, it would be over. He drank down his manhattan and then he threw the glass at me. He yelled for me to shut up and get him another drink.

"I mixed his drink, and I thought about what he said. He blamed me for that woman, whoever she was. She had more courage than I did, because she left him. I didn't ask if he had married her, but I don't think he had. All I knew was that this had to stop. I had to do something, or one of these days I would not survive Frank's rage.

"I could not understand why he didn't get over the wounds of the past. He never forgot being wronged, and I found that unnatural. What made him different from anyone else? Everyone gets hurt by careless words directed at them at times. For a church-going Christian to be unable to forgive those hurts was against all Christian doctrine in my view. After all, we all say things we don't mean, and sometimes we don't even realize those words hurt someone's feelings. But Frank didn't forgive and he didn't forget. He had a litany of charges against a special few, and he repeated them over and over daily.

"When I took him his drink, Frank grabbed my wrist and wrung it hard, until I cried out in pain. He told me never to question him again. I pulled out of his grip and rubbed my wrist. I could see the red prints of his fingers on it.

"Right then I knew what I would do, if not that night, then soon. And I did it."

Astrid had stopped painting, and scratched her bare arm, leaving a streak of white paint. She stared at Abram.

"Why did you close the notebook?"

"Because that's all there is. That's the end."

Though he was grinning, she could see that he was just as perplexed as she was.

"That's damned awful, Abram. We don't know what she did."

"That's about the size of it."

"Well we've got to find out. We know *she* isn't dead, so what did she do? She kill him? Surely she wasn't capable of sending him packing."

"Maybe she poured out all his liquor," Abram said.

He was close to laughing, and that was annoying. He shouldn't enjoy her frustration.

"You know she wouldn't do that. She was too timid. Besides, he'd have killed her if she had."

"I agree there. You're really upset by this, aren't you?"

"Damned right. I want to know what she did."

When Abram broke into a full laugh, Astrid stuck her finger in the paint and went for him, dragging a long white smear across each cheek, while he laughed harder.

"Hey," he yelled. "That's not fair. You're taking advantage of a cripple."

"Cripple! You're no cripple, but you keep it up and you just may end up being one."

"Don't take it out on the messenger, Astrid. I only read as far as I could. You can't blame me for that. She's the one who stopped writing. If you want to know the ending so bad, why don't you find out where she is? We can visit her."

"And do what? Ask her if she was a murderer? 'So nice to meet you, Mrs. Guilford. And tell me, did you kill your husband?'"

"I expect we might be a bit more tactful."

"As if, out of the blue, she'd simply tell us whether she murdered him. I doubt it very much."

"For the sake of argument, let's say she did him in," he said, "I wonder how she disposed of the body."

"I read a true account of a murderer in England who couldn't carry one of his victims down a flight of stairs, so he cut the body up into small pieces and flushed them down a toilet. Maybe she did that."

Astrid looked toward the powder room door.

"You think maybe that's why the drains work so slowly?" she asked.

"That's a disgusting thought. Of course she didn't do that. And the drains work slowly because the plumbing needs to be replaced."

"Well, a man's body would be pretty difficult for her to manage."

"If she cut him up, there would have been blood from one end of the house to the other. I see it different. I tell you what. You want to guess what she did? Want to make a bet?" Abram asked.

"You want to make a wager on where the body is?"

"Well, first we have to determine if there is a body."

Astrid started rolling paint again, thinking what she would do if she were in the situation that Doris Guilford was in. If she had a raving maniac for a husband who took great pleasure in punishing her for his own shortcomings with another woman, how would she kill him and then, how could she get away with it?

"I'll bet with you," she finally said to Abram. "I'll bet that Mrs. Guilford waited until he went to sleep and then walloped him over the head with a heavy skillet. Then she cut him into manageable pieces and hid the body parts somewhere. Probably in the cellar. That's where most bodies are buried."

"I had no idea most bodies are buried in cellars. Is that why most women avoid going down to a dark cellar? Too many lovers buried there?"

Astrid pointed her paint roller at him in warning.

"Hold on," he said. "You're far too melodramatic. You're really hung up on that dismembering thing, aren't you. No more crime books for you. I see a different scenario. I'll bet she poisoned him with rat poison. As much as he drank, after a while he wouldn't even notice it in a drink. Then, she rolled him up in a rug, and had the trash hauler pick it up and take it to the dump."

"You don't think the trash hauler might notice that he was trying to wrestle a dead body into his truck? The odor alone might hint that he was carrying something more than a rug."

"Well, maybe she tied it in the middle and on the ends. It would have been heavy, but she could tell the trash collectors that there were three rugs rolled into one, so they were heavy."

"But his body would have been found sometime along the way. They used open dumps back then, you know. And just what are we betting here?" Astrid asked. "Money?"

"Naw. Let's not be too materialistic. How about a good dinner at the Edge of Town Restaurant. If I win, you pick up the tab and if you win, I do."

"What if neither one of us is right?"

"Simple. We go fifty-fifty. Split the bill."

"You're on. Now, why don't you do a bit of work on

it, and get the big telephone directory in the kitchen and call the nursing homes in Bangor. She may not be there, but I bet she is."

"How much?"

"What?"

"How much you want to bet?"

"What the hell is wrong with you, Abram? You suddenly got the gambling fever? There's no bet. I was speaking rhetorically."

He left the room, mumbling something about rhetorical bets. Astrid could hear the pages being flipped over as he searched for nursing home telephone numbers, and then he was talking on the phone. When he returned, he had that smug look that he loved to assume lately when he was right about something.

"Is Friday okay with you for visiting the Country Care Nursing Home?"

"Sure. She's there? In Bangor?"

"The nursing home's just outside Bangor, and yes, she's there. The director said Mrs. Guilford is frail, but we can visit for a while. She stopped short of saying that she's on her death bed, but the way she hesitated before saying frail sounded like that's the case."

"Poor woman. Okay. Friday it is. Natalie won't mind."

Astrid stood back and looked at the wall she'd just painted.

"So, what do you think? Look better?"

"Better than what?"

Abram sidestepped the flying paint rag.

NINETEEN
TUESDAY, SEPTEMBER 5, 1989

Phones began buzzing almost as soon as the newspaper hit the stands, and though most of the questions were answered in the stories beginning on page one, caller after caller asked where and when the Zoning Board meeting would be held, whether it was an open meeting, would the board make a ruling at the meeting. Many were outraged that Secretary Randall King had acted unethically, and promised to express loud opposition to the shopping center come Wednesday evening.

By closing time, the editorial room had three slaphappy reporters, who were almost reluctant to leave after the barrage of support they'd received for excellent coverage of the proposed zoning variance that might have gone unnoticed until the Wolf farm was only a memory and bulldozers had torn into the landscape, with cement trucks waiting to pour the base for a Wonderland mall. Seldom had any of the writers felt the value of their work as they did today.

Astrid closed her top drawer and looked at the time.

"Helluva day," she remarked.

Natalie and Dee said, "Helluva day," in concert and they all laughed as if they had just yelled bingo at a high stakes game.

"Well, kiddos, see you in the morning, and we'll go home after the conference with Mr. Cornell." Natalie said. "That is, if he shows up for it."

"Ya? I never see him. Isn't he supposed to be at our conferences each week?" Astrid said.

"Supposed to," Dee said. "But he seldom is."

Natalie added, "He has little interest in the editorial end of his business. That's why he wants to sell it. Dee, you should have bought it. I suspect the offer is still open for you."

Though Dee rolled her eyes at the suggestion, Astrid thought now that she appeared less certain of that decision not to take over the newspaper. Once before, Dee turned both thumbs down when it was mentioned, unlike her tentative expression just now. There could be no doubt of her ability to operate the newspaper business, given her background in running the alcohol rehab camp as well as her knowledge of the editorial room.

They walked out together to the nearly empty parking lot. Astrid felt like a sorority sister, in a way, saying goodnight to two of her best friends.

She stopped to pick up the pizza she had ordered, and drove to Lilac Lane, anxious to dig into that cheesy concoction with the tantalizing aroma. She was soon opening her front door, and before she had closed it behind her, she called out to Abram. His faint response told her he was feeling poorly. She took the box of pizza to the dining room where he remained in his big chair, holding his right arm to his body.

"So you saw the doctor?" she asked. "You got there on time? Did the taxi show up on time?"

"No problem getting there. A bit of a problem after I got there, though."

"You want pizza in here or in the kitchen"

"Kitchen. I can walk out there. Just feeling a bit of pain, that's all."

Astrid helped him out of the chair, and as they settled at the table, she put a slice of pizza on a dish for him.

She asked, "What was the problem?"

"I had to wait an hour in a crowded office, but I expected that. When I finally got to see Dr. Sahan, he asked several questions. Then he took off the sling and removed the stitches. He asked how high I could lift my arm, and I felt like a baby. I could barely move it. He took hold of it and moved it upward and just about lost me right there. I don't think I ever came so close to fainting. In fact, I told him to take it easy. Well, I got through it, but I had to take a painkiller just now and it hasn't kicked in yet."

"Of course it hurts. It takes a long time to get over major surgery, and you had a very bad tear. Did he tell you when you can start physical therapy?"

"I had to go down the hall and make an appointment in the P.T. department. You should see it. They have all kinds of equipment, and on the other side of the hallway is a long exercise pool. Quite something. They gave me a whole month of appointments. I get three treatments each week. And then after four weeks, I go back to see the surgeon."

"And when do you start?"

"Next Monday afternoon at one."

They fell silent as they ate. Astrid wanted to tell Abram all about her day, but he didn't need her prattle now. And, after all, it didn't amount to a whole lot, when you got right down to it, she thought. It was just that she and the others were so enthused over their own good work and the public's reaction. To tell it now would sound like boasting.

"It's good pizza," he said.

"Ya. Not the healthiest food, perhaps, but I wasn't anxious to cook something myself."

"Suits me just fine. Did you get the paper out all right?"

"I brought a copy home for you, if you feel like looking at it later. Everything went well. Had a lot of calls from those who bought it on the newsstands. There's a lot of disgust over the conflict of interest. We'll see how it plays out, but right now I'd say the Zoning Board will think twice before approving this thing."

Abram yawned and pushed his plate aside.

"I'll go back to my chair now," he said.

"You didn't feed the cat today, did you?"

"No. Haven't seen her."

Astrid picked up the dishes and cleaned the kitchen, trying to think what she should do this evening. Painting left a lingering odor that might be offensive to Abram, and she didn't want to add to his discomfort. By the time she gave thought to the cat again, it was dusk. She went to the door and called, but the she didn't come.

"Here kitty, kitty," she called louder as she walked outside and looked around the corner of the shed. Then she saw her.

"Oh dear God," she said, rushing to the furry little body lying behind the shed. She'd seen enough dead animals to know that kitty was not alive.

Instinctively, she looked toward the house at the opposite end of her property, a house that faced on Spring Street, and the one where she believed Jason Trump lived. She heard a door close next door, and looked around. It was a neighbor that she had seen only a couple of times, Mrs. Edwards. She was walking in her direction.

"Hello. I'm Margaret Edwards. I saw you from my kitchen window and thought I'd come over and introduce myself. I read your story in the newspaper today, and wanted to tell you what a good writer I think you are. We plan to...oh! Is that cat dead?"

"I'm afraid she is. I was just going to see what happened to her."

"Don't touch her. She might be diseased."

"I don't think so."

Astrid bent over and touched the lifeless body, moving the fur enough to find if she had been injured.

"Ya. There it is. She's been shot."

"Shot! No one shoots guns around here. Who would do such a thing?"

"That's what I'd like to know, and I'm damned sure I'll find out. Were you home today? Did you hear anything?"

"I'm not home days. I work with my husband. We're

accountants. We have an office in the Fairchance Savings Bank."

Standing, Astrid looked down on Margaret, a puffy woman of about forty-five, she guessed. Her flushed face suggested high blood pressure

"It's very nice to meet a neighbor, and I appreciate your coming over. We'll have to get together sometime, Margaret."

"Yes, yes. I started to say that my husband and I will be at the meeting tomorrow night. We couldn't go last week, but we feel that we need to be there to add our voice to those who want to keep Fairchance the pretty city that it is."

"That's good to hear. I'll look for you there."

"And what about your friend? Will he be going, too?"

That sounded like a probe for a bit of gossip, and Astrid turned to go back into her house. As she did, she said, "I don't think so."

Inside, she rushed to Abram, talking all the way from the back door, but she knew he'd have no trouble hearing her.

"Damned, rotten, cold-blooded murderer. What did that little kitty ever do to him? Well he's not going to get away with it."

"What are you fuming about, Astrid?"

Abram was wide awake in his chair, looking bewildered.

"I'm talking about our cat. Some damned imbecile used her for target practice. She's out in the back yard, dead. If it's that Jason guy, he'd better watch his step around here, or he'll find that he's the target next time when I aim a fist in the direction of his nose. If I knew for sure it was him, I'd call the police and have him arrested."

"Susie is dead?"

"Susie! That what you were calling her?"

"Well, she had to have a name, and when I said it to her, she meowed as if she understood."

"You're a strange one, naming a cat Susie. She'd probably have meowed if you called her Sam."

Astrid slumped into the swivel chair.

"Damn," she said. "I guess I'll have to get the shovel and dig a grave for her out back. I hate doing that."

"I'd do it, if I could."

"I know. I liked the idea of having her around. There's something comforting about an animal in the house, especially a cat. They're so soft and cuddly."

"When they want to be."

"Ya, when they want to be. Independent, sure. But as they age, they're like people. They calm down. Then they become good lap pets."

"I think I'd like a lap pet," Abram said.

His tone was seductive, and Astrid was pretty sure he wasn't talking about a cat. However, she chose to ignore the comment. It wasn't the first time she'd noticed a sexual overtone to his words, and she had to decide if she wanted him to be excited by her presence or not. Certainly not if all he had in mind was remaining in her house as a lover. But all of that would be sorted out later, when he was healed and she could either tell him to go get his own apartment or give him an ultimatum.

She went to the shed and found the right spade for the job of grave digging, all the while asking herself what her ultimatum would be, if she ever got to that point. Would she say she would find someone else to do the renovations, or would she put her foot down and tell him she would tolerate no more double entendres, or might she get really stupid and tell him if he wanted a close relationship, then he could marry her?

"Good lord," she muttered to herself. "What am I thinking? He wouldn't want to marry me."

She went a distance from the house, where tall weeds and bushes had overgrown, and tested the soil to see if she could easily dig it up. Finding the right spot, she dug until it was a big enough hole for the cat. When she looked up, she found that darkness was settling in fast. It occurred to her that whoever the shooter was, she could have been a target herself. Why not? A cat or a woman to someone who didn't have a scruple about killing would be no different.

"That's a stupid thought. No one could be that crazy."

She hurried back to where the little body was, scooped it up in the shovel, and took it over to the hole. She never liked burying a pet, though she had done it a couple of times on the farm. It was shoveling the dirt over the carcass that got to her. She wondered how grave diggers for humans could do it. She felt a bit like crying or throwing up, or both.

"There," she said when she patted down the last of the dirt. "It's done. Rest in peace, Susie."

For the remainder of the evening, Abram sat with his eyes closed, while Astrid stayed in the kitchen to pay bills at the desk. Both were subdued by the needless killing of a little animal, their adopted pet.

When she heard Abram cough, Astrid left her work to see if he needed something.

"No," he replied to her query, "I'm fine. Did you bury Susie?"

"Ya. Over by the old fence. Do you think Jason did it?"

"I have no way of knowing what he might do. After all, I only saw him once."

"I just think he's the likely shooter, from the way you described him. He ought to have some bird shot fired at his backside, so he couldn't sit down for a week."

"What makes you so sure he's the one?" Abram asked.

"Because—because—well, I don't know. But I just feel it. Things were quiet here before he arrived. No one was shooting off a gun."

"It could have been some kid with a new air rifle that he got for his birthday. Boys are known to be aggressive with weapons, you know. Some kid who doesn't like cats would think it was great fun to shoot at one."

"Whoever it was, she was shot only once. If it was a kid, he would most likely shoot several times. She'd have been riddled with wounds."

Abram squinted, and Astrid could see that he didn't

agree with her. Nevertheless, Jason Trump was a man who should be watched. Abram himself said that she shouldn't let him in the house, and until she knew differently, she'd put him at the top of her list of suspects.

TWENTY
WEDNESDAY, SEPTEMBER 6, 1989

Sitting where she did last week, Astrid looked around the hearing room, astounded that it was not only crowded, but many stood in the open doorway and beyond. At the front of the room, dazed expressions on the faces of the Zoning Board members left no question as to their surprise at the voter turnout. It was ten past seven o'clock and still the hearing had not been called to order.

Conspicuous by their absence were the three Construcorp men in black, likely the reason for the delay. Secretary King fidgeted, leaning first to the two board members on one side for a whispered conference, and then to those on the other side. Five more minutes went by, while the noise level increased as impatient residents waited.

One man stood up and called, "What are we waiting for, the first snow?"

Around Astrid, similar comments were going around.

"Why doesn't he start the meeting?"

"What's going on?"

Secretary King ignored the jeers and questions, and Astrid began to wonder if there would be a meeting at all. She glanced across the room at Dee, who was engaged in conversation with a man and his wife beside her. Then she saw Gunnar's sun-bleached hair above others around him. Gunnar saw her, too, and waved. His broad smile sparked a sense in her that he knew something no one else did. She was about to go over and speak with him, when everyone stopped talking. Looking toward the desks up front, she saw that Mr. Carney had entered and was talking with board members, his back to the assembly. He held up a newspaper in front of King, and Astrid was quite sure it was *The Bugle.* Their words were hushed, but disagreement was obvious by King's waving hands and Carney's shaking head.

At last, Carney took long strides to the side door, and left.

King pulled a handkerchief from his pocket to wipe his forehead. If ever Astrid had seen defeat, she saw it now. The other board members sat with heads bent, not looking at anyone in the crowd. Finally, King stood up.

"Well, ladies and gentlemen, it seems that there has been an unexpected development."

A ripple of light laughter floated through the room, but King appeared not to recognize the pun he'd dropped.

"Mr. Carney has just informed us that Construcorp is withdrawing its application to construct a shopping center in Fairchance. This hearing is now adjourned."

A stunned silence followed while the board members filed out of the room.

Then slowly a murmur started, until a loud male voice shouted, "We won," and a victorious shout went up, breaking the moment of awe.

Astrid, Dee, and Natalie met at the back and edged out of the room, pausing at the front of the Court House to clear their heads.

"Well, that didn't take long," Dee said.

"I just knew when Carney came in that it was over," Natalie said. "I saw our newspaper in his hand. I'd say that we saved our city as we know it."

Astrid was looking over the heads of those around her, and when Gunnar raised his hand behind clumps of chatting citizens, she went to him.

"I see you made it," she said.

"Sure did." His face shone with excitement. "And I think I may have a sale for the farm."

"What? You haven't talked with them yet, have you?"

"I did. It took some doing, but I managed to reach Mr. Carney this morning. He was staying in Bangor, and he told me he'd talk with me if I could get there before noon. So, I drove right up there, and handed him a copy of your paper, Astrid. After he read some of it, he thanked me. Then I told him why I wanted to see him. I had a map with me and laid it out so he could see the layout of the farm. I pointed out that even though the farm is out a bit from major cities, it's central, too. And I explained that the area is beginning to grow with more businesses setting up in the neighboring towns because of lower taxes, and that it's bound to attract more homeowners to come live there, for the same reason. All in all, I did a damned good job of selling the idea to him."

Astrid listened with interest, but still couldn't believe

that a shopping mall would be set up in the middle of nowhere. However, to discourage Gunnar now would be unkind. Better let him bask in a bit of optimism while he could.

"Did Mr. Carney say he'd buy the farm?" she asked.

"No, but he did say he'd come take a look at it."

"When is he going to do that?"

"I don't know. He'll be in touch as soon as he can."

"Oh Gunnar," she started to sound a negative note, but changed her approach. "I hope for your sake that it works out."

"Thanks, Astrid. Maybe I'll get free of the farm after all. And you thought I couldn't do it. Well, I've got to get back home and tell Charlotte. I'll let you know what happens. You can write it up for your paper."

He laughed.

"Yes, Gunnar. You let me know."

Astrid watched him practically run along the sidewalk and cross to the parking lot, and though her heart ached knowing that he was due for a terrible let-down, she was glad to see him happy for just a while, at least.

* * *

Abram was at the table, reading an old book he'd found among Mrs. Guilford's left-behind items and listening to country music on the radio. He looked surprised when Astrid walked in at seven forty-five.

"What happened?" he asked. "You're early."

Astrid pulled a chair out and sat opposite Abram at the table.

"It's all over. We waited and waited, and finally Mr. Carney came in, had a heated discussion with the board members, and left. Then Secretary King got up and announced that Construcorp had withdrawn its application for the shopping center zoning variance. That was it. You should have seen all the people who came and how they shouted after it was over."

Setting aside the book, Abram said, "Then why aren't you happier? Anyone would think you'd lost the fight."

"Oh, just a bit worried. Gunnar was there and we talked after the meeting. He thinks he has sold Mr. Carney on the idea of buying his farm and building the shopping mall there in the Appleton area. He has such big ideas. I don't know where he got them. None of our family was that way. We all believed in hard work. But not Gunnar. He wants it all handed to him on a silver platter. I don't know. It's worrisome. You want some coffee?"

"Yeah, I'll take some. Like you told me about my brother, Gunnar isn't your responsibility, Astrid. I know you can't help thinking that you should protect your younger sibling, but he's old enough to take care of himself."

"Old enough, ya. But not responsible enough. I wonder if he'll ever grow up."

After plugging in the coffee pot, she went to the refrigerator, brought out the remainder of a cream cake she'd bought at the bakery yesterday, and cut two pieces to go with their coffee. She set the food on the table. Before she could sit down again, the phone rang.

To her surprise it was Mrs. Guilford at the nursing home.

"You asked to see me Friday," Mrs. Guilford said. Her voice shook so badly that Astrid could barely understand her.

"Yes. My friend called and made the appointment."

"Well, I wonder if you could come tomorrow, instead?"

"Just a minute, please." Astrid cupped her hand over the phone and said to Abram, "It's Mrs. Guilford. Wants us to see her tomorrow."

He nodded, and she continued to talk.

"Yes, Mrs. Guilford, we'll be happy to do that. Are you strong enough? You sound weak."

"I'll be strong enough tomorrow, but I need to talk with you. It's important."

They agreed on an afternoon visit, and Astrid hung up.

"What's that all about?" Abram asked.

"Beats the hell out of me. The coffee's ready. I'll bring it over. She just said it's important that we come tomorrow. She sounded like she was dying. Maybe you were right."

TWENTY-ONE
THURSDAY, SEPTEMBER 7, 1989

She'd spent a restless night, worrying about Gunnar, then contemplating why Mrs. Guilford needed to see them so suddenly, and occasionally thinking about Mrs. Wolf's farm and what King would do with it in the future. Now Astrid had to get up and go to work. As always, she left her bed at six, a habit from her childhood days when family ate meals together at regular hours.

Abram was part of her early morning routine, but soon he'd be able to bathe himself. Without strength in his right arm, it wasn't safe for him to use the tub yet. Astrid hadn't made a decision about bathroom renovations, whether to do them now or wait until the house was moved. In fact, the whole thing had begun to seem unrealistic to her. She had begun to think that she might not have the house moved, and in that case, she would want to have all new plumbing done soon. The only changes made so far were new appliances and microwave oven in the kitchen, as well as inside paint and the roof patching. She'd had the carpet steam cleaned so that it smelled better, even though it still looked worn. In its favor was the color, a dark tan.

After breakfast, she did the ritual bathing of Abram's upper body and helped him on with his shirt.

"I think you missed your calling," he said as she carefully slid his useless arm into a shirt sleeve. "You should have been a nurse. You're a natural at it."

"It's nothing. I helped my grandfather when he was too weak to help himself, and then my father. They both died within the space of two years, and my mother was too devastated to do much. So I got practice."

Abram touched her arm with his good hand.

"I can relate to that routine."

"Ya. You did it, too, no doubt. Unhappy times. It's so hard to lose those you love. But life goes on, and we go on, too."

Astrid buttoned the final button and stood back to look at him.

"Didn't you ever marry, Abram?"

"No, not yet."

He appeared to be uncomfortable in answering her question. Astrid understood. She had that special talent for asking the wrong questions. Surprisingly, though, he continued.

"I was engaged to marry, just before my brother got sick. I couldn't leave him much toward the end, and she found someone else who was more available, I guess. Maybe she just didn't care as much about me as…"

"As you did her?"

"Something like that."

His nervous laugh said to Astrid that, in reality, the affair had broken his heart. In a way, she was glad it did. Not that she wanted his heart to be broken, but it left him a free man, and for that she was most grateful.

"How about yourself?" he said. "You've never been married. Were you engaged?"

"Me? God, no."

Astrid ran up the stairs for one final bathroom visit before going to work, and when she returned, Abram was standing, looking around at the living and dining rooms.

"You don't want to be married?" he asked, continuing their conversation.

"I don't know. Maybe. Probably. If the right man comes along."

"What are you looking for?'

"I'm not looking for anything in particular. But if the right man comes along, I'll know it."

She headed for the door.

"Well," Abram said. "Give it some thought. You might want to define the qualities you're looking for. Otherwise, you might not recognize him when he comes along."

"Ya. Ya."

All the way to work, she thought about that discussion. Abram certainly pressed the question hard enough. But there was no need to read anything into it. Men were like that, after all. They'd just keep at it until you committed to something you might not have committed to if you had taken the time to think about it.

"I've already given it too much thought for one day. Can't dwell on nonsense all day long."

Yet for the rest of the morning at the office the vision of a broad back and strong biceps, a crooked grin and devilish eyes kept springing up like an active geyser, leaving her breathless and without ability to focus on much of anything else. She was relieved when noontime came and she could leave. Natalie had readily agreed when she asked for the afternoon off to see a dying friend in a Bangor nursing home. It was no lie, just not exactly accurate.

Back home, she prepared their usual light lunch of sandwiches and fruit, before they left for Bangor. All through lunch, neither had spoken much, and Astrid felt a sense of relief that Abram didn't pursue this morning's line of discussion.

As they lingered over coffee and cookies, Abram broke the silence.

"Can't help thinking about Mrs. Guilford's phone call. I wonder why she wanted us to come today."

"She sounded very ill," Astrid said. "I hope…well, I don't know. If she's that ill, it may be a wasted trip."

"We can always go to the mall."

"Oh ya. You would think of that. I don't want to hear about a damned mall again. I got my fill of that prospect. But I would like to go to a camera shop. It's about time I bought my own camera. I need one handy in case I should run across an accident somewhere on the road, a fire, or anything that's news worthy. I can't keep the office camera with me."

"Has anyone checked with King to find out what he plans to do with his land grab?"

Leave it to Abram to think of something that she should have done this morning. No one had mentioned getting a statement from King. She'd have to speak of it tomorrow when she was in the office again.

"Not yet. We'll be following up on the story, of course."

They left after lunch and arrived at the nursing facility at two o'clock. When Astrid told the front desk clerk whom they wanted to see, she was asked to take a seat in the waiting area. Before long, a fiftyish woman in a conservative gray dress with long sleeves came toward them.

"Astrid Thorpe? I'm Miss Rutherford, head nurse here. Come this way to my office, please."

They followed her to an airy room with tall bookcases, floor to ceiling windows, plush beige carpet, and a desk. They sat in the two chairs opposite Miss Rutherford. She folded her hands on the desk blotter.

"I'm afraid I have bad news for you, Mr. and Mrs. Thorpe."

Abram guffawed.

"We're not married," Astrid said quickly. "This is Abram Lincoln. He made the appointment with Mrs. Guilford in my name."

"Oh, I see. Well, as I said I have bad news. Mrs. Guilford has been declining in health daily. She was very weak. She died just an hour ago. I tried to reach you, but there was no answer."

"Damn," Astrid blurted. "Sorry, but we had looked forward to talking with her."

"I understand. She seemed desperate to talk with you, too. But she did leave something for you. She left instructions to give this envelope to you if she should pass on before you arrived."

Miss Rutherford stood up and stretched across the desk to hand the large manila envelope to Astrid. Intrigued by its size and curious to know why Mrs. Guilford was so well prepared with it, Astrid wanted to open it, but since it was sealed and taped, she thought better of it.

"Thank you, Miss Rutherford. We appreciate this. Mrs. Guilford must have anticipated her death, then."

"I think she did. She wanted to speak with you, but didn't tell us she also had a man coming to visit. She must have called him and forgot to tell us."

"A man visited?"

"Yes, this morning. In fact, he was the last one to see her alive. We discovered her body about a half hour after he left."

"May I ask who it was? It might have been my brother," Astrid said, thinking that if she didn't have a good reason to ask, Miss Rutherford might not give her the name.

"I don't think it was Thorpe, but let me check with my secretary."

She went to the outer office to ask.

"No, it wasn't Thorpe," Miss Rutherford said on returning. "It was Jason Trump. Unless he's your half-brother?"

"No, but I know the name, and I do recall that he was a friend of Mrs. Guilford's. Well, thank you for talking with us, Miss Rutherford."

"You're quite welcome. I'm just sorry you didn't see her before she died."

At the office door, Astrid asked, "What did she die of, may I ask?"

"Just old age, I'm afraid. She was worn out and her heart simply stopped."

They returned to the Jeep and slid into their seats before Astrid tore open the envelope.

"Can't wait until you get home?" Abram said.

"No, I can't." She pulled a spiral-bound notebook from the envelope. "Well, look at this, Abram. It's just like the diary at home. I wonder…"

She turned to the first page.

"Yes. It is. It's more of the diary. She must have worked on it at the nursing home. Well, I won't stop to read it now, but I am anxious to know what happened. We'll read it at home."

She started up the Jeep, and they were soon on the highway headed south toward Fairchance.

"I'll just bet she didn't die of old age," Astrid said. "I wonder if the killer wanted this notebook. I wouldn't put it past that Jason Trump to have helped her cross over."

Abram studied her profile.

"You're awfully anxious to hang the worst possible actions on that man, and you haven't even met him yet. Why is that, Astrid?"

"Because you gave me reason to, that's why. You said I shouldn't trust him, and I don't. Well, just think about it. He was in the room only minutes before they found the poor woman dead. Don't you find that a bit too coincidental? I think it's damned incriminating."

"Boy, I sure hope you never find a dead anything just after I've been in the vicinity."

"Oh, please. He's lived somewhere that we know little about."

"We know a bit about South Korea, Astrid."

"Well, we don't know what he did there after the war, or why he stayed there all those years. Why didn't he come back to Fairchance after the war ended?"

"I believe it was because he got married. You know what that means. The old ball and chain kept him there."

Abram ducked.

"Very funny., Abram."

After a few minutes, he asked a question.

"Just how do you think he killed her? The nurses would have seen any marks on her if he had strangled her."

"That's not the only way to kill a person in bed."

"You think he had sex with her, and her heart stopped?"

"Abram! Stop that. Of course not. But he could have smothered her with his hand or a pillow."

"Hmm. I guess. What do you think was his motive, then?"

"Well, I don't know what his motive might have been, but I still bet he had something to do with her death. It might have been the notebook. Maybe she wouldn't tell him where it was."

"Can't see why he'd want that. And, he'd never find out where it was if he killed her, would he?"

"No. Well, I don't know. I just think he did kill her, that's all."

"So what do you want to bet?"

"There you go again with the betting thing. Really, Abram."

"You don't want to make a little wager? I'll bet you three days' free work on your house that Jason Trump is totally innocent of these killings that you say he did."

"And I'll bet you an extra three days' pay for work over and above your work week that he did both of them, the cat and Mrs. Guilford."

TWENTY-TWO

How did it happen so fast? Jason had been at the attic window for twenty minutes trying to figure out the answer to that question. He'd gone to see Doris Guilford with the intention of getting money from her. She was a rich woman. He knew that. Frank once said he'd leave his wife well off so that she wouldn't need to work.

But it all went wrong.

Her condition surprised him. Even though the nurse had told him she was very weak, he thought she'd be able to talk with him. Then he saw her, all bones and veins, her eyes closed, breathing hard, propped against two pillows. He leaned over her white head to talk quietly so no one passing the door would hear. When he did, the sour odor was almost more than he could take, but he was determined. He needed money fast.

"Hello, Doris."

She started, as if she hadn't seen him before.

"Don't be nervous now. You knew I was coming. I called you yesterday. Remember? You were talking okay then. You hear me?"

"Um."

Her pathetic voice didn't deter him. He needed money.

"You don't have to worry. All I want to know is where

the money is. All that money that Frank hid away. Where did he put it?"

"I don't know."

He was ready to shake her. Of course she knew. She couldn't have lived there all those years and not know. She worked after Frank was gone, earned wages, and didn't spend anything. That was obvious. She had no need for the money. She must have left the stash where it was. It had to be there. Unless she trusted banks. He came prepared for that possibility.

"Did you take it and put it in the bank?"

"No. I don't know anything about any money."

"Don't lie to me. You and I both know what you did. And I don't think you used that money. You either left it where it was or you banked it. If you took out an account for it, you can sign this paper, authorizing me to have access to that account. You understand?"

He held up a paper and laid it on the bed table.

"No. I don't have any money."

She was trying to tug the sheet up to her chin, but Jason yanked it down. Her emaciation was awful to see, but he'd seen as bad before. She was still talking and breathing. She would sign her money over to him.

"You want me to tell the police about what you did? You want to die with public shame against your name? I will, you know. I will go to them and they will come and question you. They'll put you in prison."

"No."

Her bony hands worked at the sheet.

He was losing patience. It should have gone easier than

179

this. She was helpless and she knew it. Why wouldn't she agree? He had a similar experience in Korea, but he was working for someone else then. That old man gave in almost at once and told him to take his money and leave him alone to die in peace. That's what he expected Doris to do. It was that simple. Unless she planned to go back home and get the money herself. Maybe that was what she planned. This could all be an act, just to make him go away.

He took a pillow from the empty bed next to hers, and held it above her face.

"You know what I can do, don't you? I can press this over your face, and you'll die. You want that?"

"No."

Though her eyes were wide open with fear, she didn't shed a tear.

"Then say yes. You'll sign the paper."

She said no more, but pressed her lips together and moved her head from side to side.

Jason's anger rose. He couldn't stay in here much longer. Someone would discover what was going on. Out of desperation, he placed the pillow lightly over her face, without pressing down.

"Now, old woman, you want me to finish this? I always thought Frank hid his money in the cellar. Did he do that? Is it in the cellar."

Doris let out a weak response that sounded like yes to Jason.

"Yes? That what you said? It's in the cellar?"

But she said no more, and he pulled the pillow away.

Now he saw a very gray, very still body with open mouth and eyes. She was dead.

"No," he whispered, "it can't be. I didn't press hard enough."

Quickly, he placed the pillow back on the other bed, straightened the covers over Doris, and stepped lively down the hallway to the exit.

As he thought about that whole scene now, at home in his attic, a foreign sensation flooded over him--fear. Doris couldn't have died from asphyxiation. He knew just how much pressure it took to kill anyone that way. She died of heart failure. And yet, he could be charged with murder if a nurse saw him leave the room and found the body just afterward. Police could arrive at his door any time, and what could he say? He left without telling anyone that she died.

That's what he should have done. He should have gone to the desk and told the nurse that he feared she died while they were talking. Why didn't he do that? He must be getting old. It's what he would have done ten years ago. Why did he panic? It was the Eye. He saw the Eye there, just like he'd been seeing it since he came back. It hovered over Doris. And he ran. How could he escape that big, black Eye that stared right into his own eyes?

He wouldn't think about that now. If the police arrived, he'd say Doris was alive when he left her. That's it. Just tell them that she said goodbye to him when he left. One thing he could do very well was lie.

Now he must get at that money. He could scratch her signature on the paper telling the bank that she authorized him to have access to her account. But he didn't even know if she ever took out an account. If she was like Frank, she didn't. Frank lost money in the bank failures back in the late twenties and never trusted them after that. Of course, she'd follow his advice.

"Hell. She may have added her own money to his in the house. She couldn't take it with her to the nursing home very well. So it must still be there."

The first thing to do was search the house. During the day Astrid worked. What about Abram? From the rear of the house, Jason couldn't see what was going on out front, so he didn't know the comings and goings. That big workshop hid everything from view. There was only one way to find out. He'd have to pay them a visit.

When he found out whether Abram left the house at all, he could plan on those times to search the house. In the meantime, he'd continue to rummage through the shed at night, just as he'd done for two nights now. Getting in and out was no problem to him since the new owner apparently hadn't found the unlocked window yet. Frank spent a lot of time in that shed that he used as a workshop, so it could be that he made a hiding place in there. So far, no amount of pushing and pulling on likely places had opened anything there. If he didn't come up with anything soon, it would mean that the money was hidden in the cellar. It was the only logical place after the shed. Not only that, but he was certain Doris said yes when he asked her if that was where the money was hidden.

"I'll go over tonight and search some more. I know there's money in that house. I just know it. And there won't be any damned cat to meow for attention."

TWENTY-THREE

As soon as she sat down at the table, Astrid took the notebook from its envelope. She thumbed through it, only to find few pages used, and at the end was a note addressed to her.

"She must have written this note yesterday," she said to Abram. "Look how shaky her hand was. I can barely make out the words."

"Why don't you make us some fresh coffee," he said, "and I'll read it aloud, if you want me to."

"Good idea. You think you can decipher the words?"

He pulled the notebook toward himself and started to read:

"Dear Miss Thorpe, I can," Abram stopped and pondered over the word can. "No," he corrected, "I *am* glad you called me."

He fell quiet, and Astrid looked over to see what he was doing.

"You having trouble reading it?"

"I'll say. Are you good at reading bad penmanship?"

"Usually. Just a minute." She plugged in the coffee maker. "There. Now, let me see it."

Again, she sat down at the table and read.

"I fear that fromone…make that someone…plans to kill me. He called me last night and trea…no…threatened me."

She stopped.

"You're right, Abram, it's terrible."

"I notice that the writing on the rest of it, leading up to the note to you, is legible. She must have written that some time ago."

"The note isn't long. I'll go on."

She took a pencil and wrote the words out, before reading to Abram again.

"Now I have it. And the coffee's ready."

After she poured them both a cup, she read from her own handwriting.

"That man is Jason Trump. If you read what I wrote in the two notebooks, you know that Jason watched that night. Now he thinks I will pay him not to report it to the police. I have no money. The nursing home is expensive, and all the money that Frank left was gone long ago. I am writing this to you now so that if I die at his hands you will make sure he is arrested for murder. Be careful. He is not to be trusted."

Astrid took a sip of coffee and closed the notebook.

"That's all she said. So, Abram, it looks like you owe me three extra days work."

"You're assuming that Jason killed her. There's no proof of that."

"It seems clear to me. He was there just before they found her dead and he had threatened her. What more proof do you want?"

"I think a confession would be in order instead of jumping to conclusions. I'll admit, I don't like the man very much, but to tag him as a murderer seems rash under the circumstances. What could he gain by killing her, anyway? He wanted money. He couldn't get it if she died."

Astrid pouted like a child. She knew Abram was right. Even so, Mrs. Guilford warned her not to trust Jason Trump, and she must have had good reason for that.

"We need to read the rest of her diary," she said. "Maybe we'll know better how to judge when we have more facts."

Abram was on his way back to his usual resting place. It was four o'clock and had been a long day. Astrid followed him into the dining room.

"You still can't lie down on your bed?" she asked.

"Not yet."

"Well, you rest. We'll read this later. For now, I think I'll go get some groceries and pay the light bill. So I'll be a while downtown. You okay now? Need anything?"

"No, thanks. I'm okay."

Downtown, Astrid parked off Main Street, behind the supermarket, and walked from there to the bakery, to buy fresh doughnuts. Morning coffee with a doughnut would be a treat.

Carrying the white bag of goodies back to her Jeep, she saw a man running across the street, straight for her, and recognized Randall King. She stood still, waiting for him to reach her, wondering what he wanted, and just a bit worried that he might want to give her a public dressing down. He'd better watch his step, she thought, or he'll find himself sitting in the ditch.

"Miss Thorpe," he said, trying to catch his breath. "I want to have a word with you."

"Here on the street? Or at your office?"

His look of disgust didn't bother her. He disgusted her, too.

"My office. Can you come over now?"

"Ya. I can. Just let me put this bag into my Jeep, and I'll walk over."

Saying no more, he went back across the street, while Astrid pondered over what he needed to say to her so urgently. It wasn't long before she was sitting in his office, waiting for him to tell her just that.

The office was small, with a window overlooking Main Street. When Astrid took out her homeowners insurance, no one had recommended the King Agency, and for that, she was thankful.

He fidgeted for a few seconds, looking at her like he'd rather be in a taut noose than here talking with her. After some throat gurgles, he spoke.

"You did me a lot of damage at our Zoning Board hearing and in your newspaper stories, Miss Thorpe."

If he expected an apology, he got none.

"Not only did you emphasize the point of ownership, which had no relevance since I would have withdrawn from the voting, but you managed to put me in such a bad light with the community that everyone in town acts like I'm a pariah."

Again, he waited for her to comment. Astrid didn't laugh, but she didn't speak, either. He alone ruined his own reputation. Creating a conflict of interest on the board was his own doing, not hers. He'd wait a long time to get an apology from her.

"The consequence of it all," he said, "is that I'm now the owner of a property that I cannot—or I should say--I don't want to support for long. I wish to sell it, of course."

Let him squirm, she thought. She had no sympathy for those who deliberately cheated and lied for their own gains.

"That brings me to the reason that I asked you to come here. You did a very good job of writing damaging articles about me and about the mall project. Now, I wonder if you can write as well about the property that I want to sell."

"Mr. King," Astrid said, "I'm not in advertising. You really should be talking with our ad manager. She can help you, I'm sure. A nice big display ad would be quite helpful. She can take photos and..."

"I want more than that," he interrupted. "I'll pay for an ad, but I think you owe it to me to write a story. You can even say that I find myself in an awkward situation, if you want. I don't care. I just need to get that property sold, and soon."

This was an interesting twist. Astrid studied King's face and saw that, despite an attempt at remaining cool, he was quite flushed. His sharp features were so tight that he looked like he was sucking an ice cube every time he breathed out through his open mouth, and his pale eyes darted about barely lighting on her once in a while.

"You want a feature story, then. Well. It's a lovely

farmstead and the land is fertile. You didn't pay a very high price for it, though."

"High enough."

He stopped, obviously realizing that he said that a bit too hastily.

"I thought it was a fair price to pay the woman," he added.

"And then you'd have doubled the price to Construcorp."

"It wouldn't have been double. Yes, it would have been a profit. But she wanted to sell anyway. I knew that she wanted to retire, and it was a chance for her to have a quick sale."

How could he possibly think she would approve of that? How could he think she'd write a favorable story about his desire to sell after all that was revealed, and after her own challenge to him at the meeting? Astrid could not suppress a smile.

"I find it damned amusing that you resort to me now for help."

"You don't have to gloat. You won, you and your colleagues."

"The public won. Voters had more to do with winning, as you put it, than the newspaper did. Of course, had the public not known about the hearing, it could have been clear sailing for you, and you could have made a bundle, even if not double, on the sale. Our part in all of it was to inform the public. They had a right to know and to express themselves."

He swiveled his chair away from the desk. Astrid took

no pleasure in anyone's trouble, but she just couldn't feel sorry for this man.

Turning back, he said, "You won't write a story? You know what the place is. You know that it's a desirable farm property."

"I surely do. Indeed. Ya, it should be purchased by someone who is interested in preservation, not destruction."

"Look at it however you want to. You think it's easy for me to ask you, of all people, for help? I'd rather walk over hot coals. But I can't hold onto that place. I need to sell it. And soon."

"What do you expect to sell it for?"

He now looked at her square on, as if seeing her for the first time.

"I want five hundred thousand for it."

"That's one hundred fifty more than you paid."

"It is. But I need to pay a lot of interest on the loan. That's the truth of it, not that I want that in any story."

"Your creditors loaned you money without security?"

"No, not exactly. But I don't want to lose everything. I'd have to go through bankruptcy if I don't sell it soon."

"I see."

All at once, she did see. Here was a chance to do something she would like to do. Not write about him and his sale, but...no, she mustn't be hasty. Was it possible that she could own that farm? It would mean a whole new way of life, and turn her plans upside down. The picture of becoming a successful agriculturist like her grandfather was flashed through her mind. Why not? She learned from him. Unlike Gunnar, she observed and absorbed everything that was going on. But now wasn't the time to speak of it.

"Let me sleep on it, Mr. King. I may be able to help you out after all, but I would like to have the weekend to consider everything. For one thing, my editor has to approve such a story."

For the first time, she spoke softly and sincerely.

"I don't think you'll have to go through bankruptcy. I'll come to your office Monday morning. What time can you see me?"

"I'll make the whole morning available to you." He spread his hands wide."Come when you like."

Outside, she felt like throwing her handbag in the air and shouting,Yes!

TWENTY-FOUR
FRIDAY, SEPTEMBER 8, 1989

Because Abram was so worn out when Astrid got home yesterday, she put off telling him about Randall King's request for her to write a feature story to help him sell the farm. Now at breakfast she related details of the meeting between the two, omitting only the part about her thought that she might buy the farm herself. Until she had the negative aspects sorted out, as well as the positive, she thought it best to delay revealing more. The positives were all too obvious, and she could barely think of anything else except owning an agricultural operation and living in that beautiful home. It was, after all, her dream home. But there were financial considerations, taxes, agricultural plan, farm staff to consider.

"So are you going to write the story?" Abram asked after hearing her account of King's request.

"Perhaps. I have the weekend to consider it. I'll see what Natalie thinks of it. You know, King was pathetic, groveling like he did. It just about killed him, but I understand why he asked me. He knows that a story is far more effective than an ad. But it's surprising that he didn't get a Bangor reporter to do it, someone who hadn't exposed his underhanded dealing, maybe."

Abram placed his hand over hers where it rested on the table next to him. The move startled her.

"Face it, Astrid. He knows who can give him the best story. You may have taken him down, but he knows that you can also help him. Of course he'd ask you. Everyone at the meeting will realize that he ate crow to come to you, and in a way, it's like he's apologizing to the general public. After all, he is in business here. He can't afford to lose his customers."

"He did say he was being treated like a pariah now. Well," she got up and began clearing the table, "Natalie is apt not to approve of a story about his farm being for sale. She may think that he can damned well pay for an ad and let it go at that. I thought that at first. But then…"

She stared out the window over the sink. She would love to run the idea of buying the farm past Abram, but he had no claim on her. Even though he'd become her confidante since moving in, he wouldn't be with her forever, so she needed to make up her own mind. The first step was to talk with her accountant and determine how they could set it up to best advantage for tax purposes.

And then there would be this house to sell. Renovations would change drastically. There would be no need to be so extravagant in upgrading it. Just make it appealing for the sale.

"Astrid? Something bothering you in particular?"

She started at Abram's voice.

"Oh, no. I was just thinking about what I need to do this weekend. That's all."

* * *

For a Friday, the office was very busy until nearly noon. Dee had left to gather news from the schools and the police and sheriff's blotters.

Now that they were alone, Astrid told Natalie about the chance meeting she had with Randall King and his request for coverage on the farm for sale.

"Oh my God," Natalie said. "I can't believe it. The nerve of that man. Is he trying to tell us how to operate our newspaper now? He thought he could get away with usury and make himself a huge profit through his connection on the Zoning Board, now he thinks he can snap his fingers and we'll run to his aid in selling property that he shouldn't have bought in the first place if he didn't plan to live there himself."

"Well, it wasn't exactly usury," Astrid said quietly.

"No, maybe not. But it wasn't kosher, either. No, we won't be catering to his 'poor me' attitude. He fell on his face because he tripped himself up. We have nothing to apologize for, nor do we write stories with a sales pitch just because someone wants us to."

Astrid waited for Natalie to calm down before launching her next news.

"I had no intention of writing the story. Just thought I should tell you what he said before letting you know what I think I'll do."

"What's that?"

"I'm thinking I'll make an offer on the farm myself. I'd like to own it."

She had Natalie's full attention.

"You! You want to buy the farm? Whatever for? Don't tell me you want to turn around and offer it to Construcorp yourself."

Astrid laughed at the thought.

"Of course not. I like farming. If I got along better with my brother, I might have stayed on our family farm and helped him. But I knew if I did, I'd be doing all the work and he'd be off gambling or cruising. I do love the newspaper work. But I can run a farm and write, too. Maybe be a correspondent or just part-time writer for you?"

"We'll work that out later. But can you finance it, Astrid?"

"I don't need to finance it. I can pay without a loan. In fact, I wouldn't want to have a mortgage. My grampa never had a mortgage, and he became very rich. I learned how to do it from him. Well, I should qualify that. He came to this country with quite a bit of change. His parents left him money."

Natalie's mouth opened as if she would say something, but closed when no words came out. Astrid laughed.

"I should mark this down on the calendar. You're speechless, Natalie."

They laughed together then, but Natalie still had that 'I can't believe it' look. Finally, she found her voice.

"All I can say is good luck. Personally, I can't imagine operating a farm, but if anyone can do it, I know you can. A farm. My goodness. Did you tell King this?"

"No, I wanted time to speak with you first, and then my

accountant. I told King that I'd see him Monday morning, and he thinks it will be to agree to writing his story."

"What a surprise he'll get." And Natalie laughed again.

"So you won't be upset if I do this? You can find someone else as a permanent replacement?"

"Sorry to say this, Astrid, but there's always someone to take this job. It looks like I'll have a full shake-up, with you and Dee both leaving. I'll miss you both. It's possible that Beth will want to return. She's on maternity leave."

"What I need is a bit of time to see my accountant. I was hoping you could do without me this afternoon after two o'clock."

"Go, with my blessing. It's incredible, but I want to see how this all turns out. Will you have help? You'd have to. How many will be working for you?"

"I think Mrs. Wolf had four or five until recently, probably part-time help. One is a farm manager, and I'd definitely keep him on. I can see that he knows what he's doing. And he has a house on what was a separate farm, but now it's all one since our friend King bought it. That made it nearly a hundred acres, about eighty percent fields. I'm not quite sure of those figures, but they're close, I think."

"It will cost a lot of money. I had no idea you were that wealthy, Astrid."

"I know. I look like a pauper most of the time."

"No you don't. It's just that I thought you needed this job to pay for the renovation of your new house. And what will become of that?"

"I'll sell it after we bring it up to date."

"I see. Well, you do what you have to do. Take more time, if you think you'll need it. Take the whole afternoon. Not much is going on here today."

That was all she needed, and Astrid said she'd do that. At noon, she went home to have lunch with Abram, but still she wouldn't tell him about her plan. She didn't need his input, and she didn't need his disapproval, if he was inclined to be disapproving. No, this was her deal, and hers alone. She had the money, and she had the know-how. No one, not even Abram, could understand how much she wanted to have her own farming operation and to live in that antique house that had the sweet aroma of old wood and spoke of a bygone era when craftsmanship was more important than hasty production. It was definitely not a Sears model home.

With that thought, she looked about at the mail-order house she now owned. It was likely better built than most modern homes, she thought, but lacked the character of the antique, where every door and window frame, every cornice, every chair rail was detailed with curves and angles to please the eye.

"You seem preoccupied a lot lately," Abram said. "You sure nothing's wrong?"

They had devoured their sandwiches and were now lingering over coffee and blueberry tarts.

"Wrong? Oh no. Nothing's wrong. Just thinking about work assignments, that's all."

"Something interesting?"

"No. Not really."

"For nothing interesting, you're putting a lot of thought into it."

"A person has to think once in a while, Abram. Don't be so damned curious."

"I didn't think I was being damned curious. I just wanted to say more than two words before you took off again."

"Oh. Well. How's your shoulder today?"

"It seems worse today, to tell the truth."

"Did you take a pain pill?"

"No. Not yet. If it gets so bad I can't stand it, I will. I don't want to sleep. Thought I might take a walk around the back lot and see what's all around us."

There he went with that *us* stuff. She didn't care what was around *her*, but he had to find out what was around *us*. The references to us and ours seemed to come out of him more and more often, as if he had a stake in this place. Well, he didn't, and one of these days she'd tell him he could stop the *us* and *we* business.

"Be careful out there. The ground's uneven," she said, instead of expressing her thoughts. "You could stub your toe on a rock or gopher hole and break the other arm."

"That would be a sight, wouldn't it? Me running around with both arms in a sling."

She laughed, thankful for a change in her own attitude. Whatever got into her, thinking like that? He didn't mean anything by his expression of togetherness, and she knew it. She really was uptight about that farm. But she couldn't tell him. Not yet.

TWENTY-FIVE

Her appointment was for two o'clock, and it was now one, giving her an hour to spare. Astrid had time to see Chris Wolf for information she would need for the accountant. Driving along the road in front of the house and barn complex, she felt excitement like she never felt, even after sinking the basketball two-pointer for the women's record win. This agricultural project would be a real, meaningful contribution to society. This was the home and the work she could love.

There had never been a question of why she didn't stay with her brother and care for the family farm. She had wanted a college education and a chance to play college basketball. She had a desire to write, as well, and that all figured into the decision to leave his farm even though Gunnar would have liked it if she had stayed and helped him. She still loved the independence farm life provided through self-sustaining food production. Caring for animals in winter was no fun, and she hadn't made up her mind whether to get into milk production or stick with crops. However, she wouldn't need to work with the animals. The farm manager would take care of that end. It was only one of many questions right now, all of which would be addressed later.

She drove to the side porch and parked, again

taking time to survey the house itself. Memory had not exaggerated its uniqueness.

"So lovely," she whispered.

Chris came out the door and called.

"Miss Thorpe. You're back again. Anything wrong?"

"Not at all. In fact, you may be quite interested in what I'm going to tell you."

* * *

Wallace Betz looked up from the account books that Chris Wolf had provided. He nodded approvingly, and Astrid relaxed.

"Looks like a well managed farm, Miss Thorpe. Now that I see the figures, I'm surprised she sold the property at such a low price. Anyone wanting to go into agriculture for a profit would have purchased at a higher price."

Astrid felt the pride of ownership, as if it were her own operation that he praised.

"I worked with my grandfather", she said, "and learned what to do and what not to do in order to realize as good a profit as possible. I learned how to save and invest, to watch the weather and the markets, and to live modestly. In other words, he taught me how to manage a farm. It's hard work, but I'm not afraid of that."

"I admire your courage to take it on," Betz said, "and it would appear that you know what you're talking about. So you want to set up a plan that will give you the most favorable tax credit possible. Well, that's no problem. Just what do you want to do different than is now being done? Anything new?"

"Yes. I noticed that the adjoining farm acres aren't in production, and I believe they should be planted with something that will give a good return on the investment, like berries. Maybe strawberries, and/or raspberries or high bush blueberries for pick-your-own sales. We could have a whole separate operation on that section of the farm, and..."

Betz held up his hand for her to stop there.

"You have a good head on your shoulders. I can see that. Go ahead and purchase the farm, then come to me again. In the meantime, I'll work up an accounting plan that you may follow. There are guidelines concerning agricultural production, and filing for tax breaks. But we'll go over all that later."

"Sounds good to me."

Astrid left the office with a great desire to go to Randall King's office and make her offer to him right now. But, she had set Monday for their meeting, and that's when it would be done. Mustn't act overly anxious, she told herself. Give him a couple more sleepless nights. Serves him right.

Since she didn't want to return home at this early hour, she returned to the office to share her decision with both Natalie and Dee. But when she arrived, she found unexpected activity.

TWENTY-SIX

In the hallway, she heard their excited voices, not shouting, just a monotone that sounded urgent. Something was wrong. Astrid walked into the office and found that Sheriff Knight was standing next to Natalie's desk. Wearing a worried expression, Dee kept her eyes on the officer, as if transfixed.

"He has always been a very private person," Natalie said. "He never told us about his wife. I didn't even know he was married. How did this happen? Where is Mr. Cornell now?"

Astrid took it all in and wondered how much she had missed and what it was that she had missed.

"The Cornells lived high on a mountain," the sheriff said, "and were driving down the mountain road. An overnight rain left the pavement slick as ice. Mrs. Cornell was in the passenger seat and Mr. Cornell was driving. He apparently tried to avoid a deer in the road, but it looks like he hit it with his Caddy, and the car swerved to the right. Skid marks tell us that he braked hard, and lost control on that slippery pavement. The car went over the side of the roadway, down a steep incline, and smashed into a large oak tree crushing the passenger side. The wife died instantly."

Astrid said, "Oh my God. How awful."

Dee's face drained of color. She looked as if she had lost her own sister.

"Poor Rebecca," she said.

"Rebecca?" Natalie said. "You knew her, did you Dee?"

"I did meet her. I couldn't very well break a confidence, Natalie. I'm sorry. It's what Mr. Cornell wanted. You know how careful he was to keep his private life private."

"You'll have to tell me about it later. For now, Larry, give me all that you have, and we'll print a story next week. I hate having to expose his life in this way, but this is public record."

The sheriff sat down in the chair beside Natalie's desk and gave her more details.

"It's tragic," he said. "The maid said Rebecca Cornell was a paraplegic. We don't know where they were going, because he's still unconscious at the Bangor Hospital, at least he was when I checked over an hour ago. When we know more, I can fill you in before your deadline, I think. To tell the truth, I don't know how he survived the crash. The car was demolished."

"Do you have any idea how badly he's injured?"

"No, but you can check with the hospital. They couldn't give me anything when I talked with the attending doctor, Dr. Lind."

"When did the accident happen?"

"Probably around eight this morning. The maid saw the dead deer as she was driving up the road and stopped. She looked around and noticed the path of the car through trees and saw auto parts. That was about nine o'clock. She said they had told her not to come early because they were going to be away for the day, and all she would have to do was wash and iron a few clothes. She didn't have to tend to Rebecca like she usually does."

Astrid listened to the horror of the accident, and remembered that Natalie and Dee had lost the reporter who held her position before she came aboard. That was an auto accident, too, and only a couple months ago. This must be terribly hard for them.

She also remembered the two times she had seen Mr. Cornell. She imagined that he was a good husband. What dreadful news he'd wake up to hear at the hospital. If he did wake up.

She looked at Dee, who had buried her face in her hands. Apparently she knew the boss well. How odd that she knew Mrs. Cornell and Natalie didn't. Why was that? Then Astrid remembered that Dee had been approached to buy the newspaper and declined the offer. Maybe that was it. Maybe she went to their home to talk it over. Must have been that. And why was he so secretive? Seemed to her that he should have been open with everyone about his wife. What possible reason would he have for not revealing such a thing? Was he ashamed of his wife's condition? That didn't really fit the personality of the man she met. At least, she didn't think it did. Astrid sank deeper into her own thoughts about the mystery of Marvin Cornell, so much so that suddenly she realized the sheriff was about to leave.

He opened the door to go.

"How are Beth and the baby?" Natalie asked.

"They're both doing just fine. Thanks for asking. Come over sometime."

If he wanted to boast about how cute the little one was, he said no more. This wasn't the moment for brightness, even though Astrid would have welcomed a lighter note right now.

Natalie looked across their desks to ask Dee a question. She couldn't hide her pique.

"Did you think I'd blab about his wife if you told me, Dee?"

Dee's eyes were watery, but she sat up straight and spoke in a strong voice.

"Of course I didn't think that. But Mr. Cornell made me promise not to speak of his private life, his home, or his wife. I saw them a week after I was rescued from Bart Tunney. They invited me to that mountain home the sheriff spoke of. I knew he would ask me then for an answer to whether I'd take over the newspaper, and I had made up my mind not to. But even before I went there, he almost threatened me when he said I must not say anything to anyone."

Natalie tapped a pencil on the desk as she weighed Dee's words. At last she tossed the pencil aside.

"I expect he did. I tried a couple of times to ask about his personal life, and always got that look that told me I was treading on thin ice. I'm not blaming you. Well, now the world will know. I wonder when they were married and why he felt that he needed to keep her a secret. I've never talked with anyone who said a word about her."

"He said she wanted it that way. She was shot ten years

ago when she happened to be in a bank that was held up, and that paralyzed her legs. But she wasn't afraid of the world. He said she wanted peace and quiet in order to compose music and to paint. She was a talented, lovely woman, and so…so…"

Dee's voice broke on the next word. "…brave. I can't believe she's gone."

"Oh God," Astrid said. "What if *he* dies? What will become of the newspaper then?"

"I have no idea," Natalie said. "We'll just have to cross that bridge when and if we come to it. For now, I'll call the hospital and see if we can get some idea of how seriously he's hurt. Dee, the sheriff said the remains of his car were hauled to Sammie's Garage. Will you go over there and take a few pictures of it? Astrid, we must have a photo of Mr. Cornell on file. Find everything you can about him and write it up."

Neither Dee nor Astrid left until after Natalie called the hospital. When she finished talking with the doctor, she said, "He has a concussion, and a cracked rib, as well as multiple cuts and bruises."

She thought for a few seconds before going on.

"Dee, since you seem to have a closer relationship with him than I do, will you go to the hospital tomorrow and talk with him? We have no information on his wife, and should write something special for her, in addition to the obit. You know what to ask—her schooling, where she spent her childhood, where and when they were married. We'll need to know her family survivors. The usual. Maybe he didn't want anyone to know about his private life, but he has no choice now. I wouldn't press him about the accident, just about the more pleasant side of Rebecca's life, as well as his own. I don't know much more than the fact that he inherited the newspaper and commercial printing operation from his father. Get him to open up, if you can."

"Sure. I'll do that."

Astrid went through the rest of the day in a daze. Her wonderful news had certainly been trumped. Instead of being a beautiful day, it turned into a black and sad one. It would be comforting to talk with Abram after all this.

TWENTY-SEVEN

She got home at five-thirty, only to find that the house was empty. Abram had no physical therapy and he wasn't driving his truck yet. In fact, it wasn't even here. He'd left it behind the hardware store for safekeeping until the doctor said he was ready to drive again. He'd been terribly restless the past couple of days, so maybe he went for a walk. She relaxed with that thought, and began to prepare supper. He would come along very soon now.

But he didn't. When he wasn't home at six, she sat down and ate her meal. Then, at seven, she picked up the phone to call the hospital emergency room. They had no Abram Lincoln there.

At seven-thirty, she was worried beyond all reason. She had no way of knowing where to start. Maybe the hardware store. He seemed to be good friends with Jake. She was about to dial, when the front door opened.

Abram called out, "Astrid. Sorry to be so late."

Her instinct was to shout, Where the hell have you been? But at the very last moment she reasoned that she had no claim on him. She must act as if she had expected him to be late, as if she just didn't care.

"Where the hell have you been?" popped out anyway.

"Ah. Was the little woman worried about me?"

Before she said any more, she saw that he wasn't alone.

An older man, who looked about ready to keel over, had followed him into the hallway. If he was of sound mind, it didn't show in his bloodshot eyes and weaving stance.

"Who's this?"

"Oh, Astrid, meet Jason Trump. He drove me around a bit. This is Astrid, Jason. As you can see, Jason, she's a diamond in the rough."

Astrid stood like a wall in front of them. Her mind told her to relax, but her emotion was wound tightly, ready to spring in a flurry of words.

"So nice of you to bring Abram home, Mr. Trump," she said as politely as she could muster. "Perhaps you can visit another time when it isn't so late in the day."

"Very nice to meet you, Astrid. Abram's been telling me about you. You've got quite a nice place here. I'd be happy to..."

"Jason," Abram interrupted. "I think this isn't the time to go into it. Like she said, come back another time."

"Oh, sure. I'm just across the way, if you need me any time. I lived in South Korea, you know. Always been good with my hands. People loved me there. But Fairchance is the pot of gold at the end of the rainbow, you know. Yeah, just a pot of gold waiting to be opened. I'm here to do just that. I'll open the pot, you better believe it."

"See you later," Abram said.

"Yeah, see you both another time, then. So very nice to meet you, Astrid. You're a beautiful woman, I must say. Abram didn't exaggerate. My wife was..."

Abram took Jason by the arm and steered him out the door.

"Goodbye, Jason," he said.

Astrid went to the kitchen with Abram following, smiling too broadly to suit her. Seeing him in that cheerful mood made her angrier. Mentally, she reminded herself to be patient and not say something she'd regret later.

"You've been drinking," she said.

"You could say that. I've had a couple of beers."

"Why? You know you shouldn't drink while you're taking painkillers."

"Oh, hell. A couple of beers don't hurt anything. I wasn't driving anyway."

"Well that crazy man shouldn't have been driving, either. Whatever got into you to go with him?"

"Jason thought I might like a ride in his new car. You should see it. It's a big black Lincoln. Anyway, I was sick and tired of sitting around this empty house. Then, we passed a barroom, he invited me to go in with him and have a couple of friendly drinks. What time is it anyway?"

"It's time you got your supper from the refrigerator and heated it up, if you want to eat. I'm going upstairs. See you in the morning."

"Well, wait a minute. Why are you so mad?"

"Because while you were with that lunatic, having a friendly drink or two, you worried the hell out of me. I thought you'd been in an accident, or something."

"You worried about me, huh? I guess that means you care."

"Idiot. I don't care what you do. I just…don't care."

"It seemed like a good idea at the time. I'd been cooped

up here about as long as I could stand it, and he gave me a chance to get out of the house for a couple of hours."

"Did he! I'm glad to hear it. Like I said, I don't care."

She threw up her hands and headed for the stairs.

"And don't you dare leave that kitchen a mess when you're through."

This was something she didn't know about Abram. He drank. Well, she wouldn't have it. In the morning she'd let him know that he'd have to go elsewhere. She would not tolerate a drunk in her house.

She sat atop the blanket on her bed and picked up the copy of *Agriculture Today* magazine she'd bought on her way home. Leafing through it while her anger sputtered to low flame, she realized just how much she had worried about Abram. Of course she cared, but why would he go out to a bar with that killer Jason Trump? But of course, she knew the answer to that. He didn't think Jason was the killer. Well, she did think so. Now that she'd met him, she was convinced of it. Just look at his rat's eyes, all beady and blank. No one would convince her that he wasn't capable of murder.

Downstairs Abram was making a lot of noise with pots and pans. What the hell was he doing? All he needed to do was pop his plate into the microwave oven and warm it up. Why all the noise? If he thought she was going down to investigate, he was mistaken. He had heard her. If he left the kitchen in a mess, she'd...what *would* she do? Kicking him out was about all she needed to do, and she was going to do that, for certain.

Where would he go? Well she couldn't let that concern

her. This was her house, not his. She'd been good enough to let him stay with her while he got over the injury, but that didn't mean that this was his house now. No. He would be out of here. Tomorrow.

Maybe she was upset more because she wanted to tell him all her news than that he'd been drinking. She didn't approve of drinking. Still, she wanted someone to talk with about Mr. Cornell and his wife. She had even been in the mood to tell him about her plan to buy the farm.

But not now. No way was she going to discuss anything with him now except his departure. She wouldn't have a man like Frank Guilford in her house or near her. Poor Doris Guilford suffered because of her husband. No man would take advantage of Astrid Thorpe, not by a long shot. Nip it in the bud, right now, that's what she intended to do.

Her thoughts about Mrs. Guilford reminded her that she hadn't yet read the last part of the diary. Where did she put it? She looked on her night stand, but it wasn't there. Did Abram have it? Had he read it? As much as she wanted to go down and ask him, she wouldn't. It could wait until tomorrow, just like everything else. She started to read her magazine, but couldn't settle down to concentrate. The more she tried to ignore it, the more she wanted to get that notebook and read more of it.

Finally, she gave in. Trying not to step on the creaky spots, she went down the stairs. The notebook wasn't in the dining room or the living room. It had to be in the kitchen, and Abram was still there. Oh well.

He looked over at her when she entered. She wanted

to laugh at him as he tried to wash dishes with his one good hand. He had splattered water all over himself and the floor. If ever there was a mess.

"You find your supper all right?" she asked.

"I did. Thank you, Astrid. As always, you were so kind to think of me."

The nerve of him, patronizing her.

"Ya. Go to hell, Abram."

She found the notebook on the desk where she had left it after returning from the nursing home. Maybe he hadn't read it yet.

When Abram saw that she meant to take it back upstairs with her, he sounded genuinely remorseful.

"I was hoping we could read that together. I'm sorry, Astrid. Honest, I'm not a drinking man, but once in a while I do like a beer. I've never been drunk in my life."

She made a sucking noise as she ran her tongue over her teeth.

"I just wish you hadn't gone with Jason Trump. He was loaded enough. He shouldn't have been driving. And you shouldn't have ridden with him. I don't trust that man."

"You're right on all counts. But I didn't realize how much he'd had to drink until we were on the road. Anyway, it won't happen again. I'm not sure I trust him, either. He had a lot of questions about our living accommodations, when you leave for work, and when I go to therapy. He thinks he'll come over and help with the renovations."

"Really. Well, he's got another think coming. Just

because you've become buddies, it doesn't follow that he can come in and do what he pleases in my house."

"I had already decided I wouldn't become buddies with him. If he comes over again, I'll let him know he's not welcome."

Abram stood with his hand in the dishpan, swishing water over a plate and looking downcast now.

"I wonder. Can we bury the hatchet?"

Astrid felt her resolve melting into nothingness. Abram was someone she could trust, and she knew it. Holding a grudge against him now would undo all her plans. Besides, she liked him. That was the truth of the matter. Sulking and acting like a child because he had a bit of an outing for a change would prove nothing except that she was an unforgiving and possibly vindictive woman, which she was not.

"Ya, we can. I just don't like liquor, that's all."

"I won't forget that, I assure you."

She raised an eyebrow.

"Here, let me do those dishes before you flood the place. You need a dry shirt."

He went to the hallway closet and came back with a long-sleeved blue cotton shirt.

"I'll help you with that in just a minute," Astrid said.

There was only the silverware to dry. With that done, she went to his side and helped him off with the wet shirt and on with the dry. It was always a temptation to give him a kiss after this process. Even now, though she had been so angry with him, she felt like leaning in and kissing him on the cheek.

"That feels better," Abram said. "Wet clothes are clammy. Thanks."

She stood looking into his eyes. They were clearer now and his grin was gone.

"Let's go into the other room, and I'll read to you," she said.

She hadn't forgotten all that she wanted to tell him, but for now it was best to settle down and wait until tomorrow before saying anything. Although Doris Guilford's diary wasn't exactly bedtime reading, both were curious about what she did and how she did it.

Astrid settled into her swivel chair and began reading the final chapter in the diary:

"My resolve to kill my husband grew stronger after I first thought of it. At first I thought I could not go through with it. Then all I thought about was how and when to do it. And that night as I mixed his drink it came to me.

"The next day he had a job to do in the country and said he would be there most of the day. After he left the house I went to his workshop. I had seen a jug of anti-freeze under a bench. It was still there and half empty. A couple months before that I had read a report about a dog that died from lapping up spilled anti-freeze. The report said animals like it because it's sweet. I didn't know how much would kill a man, but decided to try it anyway. I had nothing to lose."

Here, Astrid stopped.

"My God, Abram. Anti-freeze. I should think that

would taste awful. How could she get enough into him to kill him?"

"I guess you'd have to read on to find out," Abram said, with no attempt at hiding his annoyance over the interruption.

Just as eager to learn the outcome of Mrs. Guilford's plan involving anti-freeze, she continued reading:

"He came home in time for supper and said little to me except to complain that the potato salad had too much onion. I had put a lot of onion in the salad and also served stuffed peppers so he would have a strong taste in his mouth before he had his first drink. He left the table and yelled at me to fix him a drink. He needed something to take the onion taste out of his mouth. I made him one drink and he downed it quickly and demanded another. Three times this happened, and on the fourth drink, I reached for the bottle I'd filled with anti-freeze and poured in half as much of it as I used of whiskey. I added a bit of vermouth and the concoction was ready. I smelled it before I turned around and took it to him. The drink smelled sweet, but I couldn't recognize the odor of anti-freeze. I tried not to look at him when he drank it. This was one of the nights that he drank fast. That meant that he planned to drink a lot. Already I could see the change coming over him. His voice had been easy enough early in the day, but now he growled with each word, and I knew it would not be long before he would find a reason to hit me. I had lived with him long enough to read the signs. He began to complain about the man who cheated him once ten years ago, then he went back to his boyhood and how he had to earn a few pennies by shining boots. These were old familiar stories and he always told about the boots covered with horse manure that he had to clean. He recalled his father who left him alone for weeks at a time to work in the woods. His angry words grew louder and louder. He got up and paced the floor, staggering slightly. He said he wanted me to stay there where I was. He said I could wash dishes in the morning when he left. I asked him if he had another job and he said he was going to Bangor where he could get some special tool he needed for his next job. I don't remember what he said it was. I barely listened because I was watching him gulp that deadly drink. To my surprise he threw the glass on the floor and demanded another. I thought I must not have given him enough, so I mixed up a drink with just a bit more anti-freeze.

"He made a face and said it tasted funny. I did not know what to say to that. If he didn't drink it, I would have to cut back on the anti-freeze in the next one. But he did drink it. This time he started talking funny. He said he thought the cat was outside. We didn't have a cat. Then he began to mumble things that made no sense. He tried to put his hand on the arm of the chair, but it kept slipping off, and he dropped it to one side of the chair seat. I couldn't understand what he was saying and his eyes became wild. He grabbed his head with both hands and said it hurt. Then he threw up. I had not expected that and ran to the kitchen for the dishpan. It didn't do much good. He had vomited most of it already before I got back.

"I asked him if he wanted me to help him upstairs to go to bed. He stood up but his balance was worse and before he got to the stairs he went to his knees and laid down on the floor. I asked him if he wanted a blanket over him so he could sleep there. I couldn't understand his answer, so I ran upstairs and took a pillow and blanket off the bed. After he seemed comfortable enough, I got a bucket and rags to clean up the mess on the living room floor. After about an hour of moving around on the floor he went to sleep.

"I don't know how long I sat in a chair just watching him. I must have dozed off myself. When I came to I could see that his face was gray. I looked at the clock. It was three-thirty. I got up the courage to feel for a pulse and could not find any. I knew he was dead. Now I had to hurry to get the rest done before daylight.

"The day before I had dug up a large plot behind the house and when my neighbor came out to hang her clothes on the line she asked me what I was doing. I told her I was going to plant a pine tree and it should be delivered within the next day or two. She asked why Frank didn't dig it up and I told her he was having trouble with his back again.

"The only way I could get the body out to that burial spot was to roll him onto a rug and pull it. By the time I tugged that heavy weight out to the plot, it was nearly dawn. I couldn't stop to rest. I rolled him into the hole and threw the rug over him, then I shoveled the dirt in and leveled it. I had to plant a tree, so I dug a hole beside the grave. I was careful to remove whole squares of sod and place them over the grave, and stomped it all down.

"I put away the shovel and came into the house. I was exhausted and fell onto the couch. It was late afternoon before I woke up. I had never been so confused. I wasn't sure if I had really done it. I walked to the back door and looked out across the field to the dug up spot. I had done it. I knew it. Now I had to call the nursery and have them bring a small pine tree to plant. They said they would deliver one the next day.

"That is how I killed the man that everyone said was so good. I have lived with this guilt for over forty years. I never felt regret. When anyone asked me about Frank, I said he had gone to Alaska. After a while I said he had an   injury and would be laid up for several months. And finally I told everyone that he died in Alaska quite unexpectedly. The pine tree grew to be huge. No doubt it got a good start from Frank's decomposing body. I looked at that tree every day and hoped that the roots had gone straight through his heart.

"I was free of a man who enjoyed hurting me in every way he could think of. Even though I knew that he was an evil man at heart, I did not correct people when they sympathized about my loss of a good man. That good man had nearly killed me more than once.

"I thought I had not been seen, but that next afternoon as I was standing by my back door, Jason Trump appeared out of nowhere. He grinned and asked how my garden was growing. I thought he might have seen me, and remembered that he had always been an early riser. I sometimes saw him out back in the early morning, just before dawn, when I couldn't sleep beside Frank any longer and went to the kitchen to make tea for myself. But Jason said no more, and the very next day he left to be a soldier in the Korean fighting."

It was a few minutes before either of them spoke. At last, Astrid said, "What a terrible thing. How could she do all that and be happy about it? She had no remorse."

"No, so it would seem," Abram said. "But she did write it all down so someone, some day, would know. It was more of a confession than a diary, wouldn't you say? Perhaps that was her way of repenting, in a way. She knew her act would come to light, and her name would be tarnished."

"A tarnished name is one thing. Could you face dying with something like that on your conscience?"

Abram thought a while, then said, "I don't know that one who has a heavy load of guilt is more fearful of dying than one who has none, because I think everyone, good and bad, is afraid at the time of death. It's the great unknown. I don't approve of killing, naturally, but I don't know what choice she had. If she lived with him much longer, there was a good chance that he would have killed her, or maybe have injured her brain so badly she'd have ended up in an institution. And like she pointed out, she couldn't get away from him and she had no one to go to for help. That's the really sad part of it all. We can judge her action as wrong. But would you have done different? Would I? I don't know. All I can say is that she had a heavy burden to carry through life any way you look at it."

"You're right. I admit, I've thought I would have killed him if I'd been her. But I probably would have found some way to escape, instead."

"Easy for you to say. You've been in the world and you have education and work skills. She had none of that going for her. She'd been a slave, first on the farm, then in her husband's house. She came to him with the anticipation that he would take care of her. He doled out very little money to her, and she had no work skills. Instead of protecting and loving her, he turned on her like a savage animal. She finally treated him like one."

"Ya. Well, now we know what happened to him."

"One other thing, though."

"What's that?"

"You owe me a dinner at the Edge of Town Restaurant."

"I do not. You weren't right, either. So how do you get that *I owe you*? No way. We split the check."

"So, you're all for that dinner anyway?"

Astrid saw the devilish gleam in his eyes, a look she had come to enjoy, even when he was getting the better of her.

"Why not? We were both right. Doris killed Frank. We were just wrong about what she did with the body."

In a more serious vein, she asked, "What do you think we should do about it, now that we know and have the evidence to prove she did it?'

"Well, we can't just let a murder that we know about go by, I guess. Maybe we should report it to the police."

"My suggestion is that we let it rest for a bit," Astrid said, "and think about it before doing anything. We might want to do some digging and see if his remains are to be found."

"And then? We opened the door to a murder when we read that diary. If we hadn't read it, we'd never have known about it."

"It is a puzzle. Poor Doris Guilford."

Astrid jumped to her feet.

"Abram. I think I know what's going on with Jason Trump. I'll bet he does know about the murder. He was up early that morning and saw her burying Frank."

"But what good would it do him to know that? Why would he go to see her? You think he killed her. Why would he do that? And after so many years."

"I don't know. It's very confusing. Oh. I *do* know. Doris wrote in the notebook that Jason thinks she had money. We still don't know why he would kill her, unless she told him where the money is. But, then, she said there isn't any."

Hunching her shoulders, she said, "It just doesn't make any sense at all."

TWENTY-EIGHT
SATURDAY, SEPTEMBER 9, 1989

Dee stepped off the hospital elevator, checked the chalk board for Marvin's name, and looked at the overhead signs for room numbers. As she walked down the hallway, she tried to gather her thoughts, but the dread she felt blocked clear thinking.

To talk with Marvin about his dear wife at a time when he was suffering so badly seemed cruel. But that was what reporters were expected to do--dig into a private life no matter what it might do to the one who was damaged. It was expected. The public's right to know. At times like this, she wanted to say to hell with that right to know business. It was cruel to infringe on a person's grief. She remembered only too well her own and how upsetting it was to answer a reporter's questions.

Gathering her courage, she walked through his open door and found Marvin Cornell, bandaged, sleeping, lightly snoring. She hesitated. This was no time to try to conduct an interview. The man was out of it. Probably they had given him a sedative. She turned to go back out. The large bag she carried brushed along the movable table and sent an empty plastic pan to the tile floor, making noise enough that Marvin woke up.

"Dee," he said. "This is a surprise. Come, have a seat."

"I hate to disturb you, Marvin. I don't need to ask how you're feeling. You're obviously in a great deal of discomfort."

"It doesn't matter."

His sigh said it all. He was hurting, but more from his loss than his own wounds.

"I guess this is a working visit," he said.

"I wish it weren't. I truly hate to ask you questions at a time like this. Let me say how dreadfully sorry I am over your loss. I find it hard to believe."

"No more than I do. Rebecca was sitting there chatting, so happy to go on a little holiday with me, when that deer ran out of the woods in front of the car. I should have just hit it, but instead I tried to avoid it, clipped it anyway, and I don't remember what happened after that. I remember Rebecca's scream, that's all. I guess I'll always remember that."

Instinctively, Dee placed her hand on his arm, wishing so much to relieve his pain. For a long few moments they said nothing. The only sounds that broke the silence were those of low voices, announcements over the loudspeakers, elevator doors rolling open and shut.

How could she approach this terrible ordeal of asking him personal questions for a page one story that would sicken him more when he read it? Well, she'd make it as easy as possible for him.

She squeezed his arm lightly.

"Maybe I should wait…"

"You ask what you need to, Dee. I know what has to be done. I've had a private life with Rebecca for a good many years. Now, it won't matter if the world knows about it. She can't be hurt any more."

"How about you?"

"Me? I've been hurt about as much as I ever can be. I have nothing to hide. I loved my wife. I kept her in a quiet place, just as she wanted, so that she could bask in the beauty of mountains and lakes and paint her lovely pictures of that scenery. She wrote her music. You know. You heard her play one of her own compositions. She was happy there as a recluse, if you will. It's not often that a person lives a solitary life for long hours of a day and finds it totally satisfying. But she did. "

He had struggled to say all that, more from pain and medication than trying to find the right words. He spoke from the heart, and Dee tamped down her own emotions, remembering those first hours of pain after learning of Barry's death.

"So, Dee, you go ahead. What do you want to know? If I think you're hitting too close to the bone, I'll say so."

"Yes. Well, I'll try to be brief. How long had you been married?"

"Twenty years. She was eighteen when I met her. I was twenty. It was a piano recital in New York. I was a student at Columbia and she was a student at Julliard. The only reason I attended was that my best friend had a girlfriend who was performing and wanted me to go with him. When I saw Rebecca and heard her play the piano, I decided to do everything in my power to get her interested in me."

He stopped to cough, and then laugh a bit. He tried to reach for the glass of water on his bedside table but failed. Dee saw that he couldn't breach the pain of an injured rib, so she held the glass to his lips, and he sipped.

"Thanks. Feels like the whole rib cage is bruised instead of just one rib. It didn't take long for us to realize that we loved each other. I sent her two dozen roses following the performance and a note asking her to have dinner with me the next Friday evening, and she accepted. When it came time for me to graduate, I asked her to marry me. She didn't even pretend to be uncertain but said yes on the spot.

"We got married in New York, had a very quiet ceremony. And we lived there for two years while I worked as a copy reader for the *New York Times*. But I was fascinated with the press room right from the start, and spent a lot of my free time there, talking with those who worked in both the composing room and the press room."

He turned his head away, and Dee thought that the session was becoming too much for him.

"Do you want me to leave and come back another time, Marvin?"

"No. It's just a hard memory, the day Rebecca went to that bank and was shot. She was just standing at the teller's window, making a withdrawal, and one of the gunmen shot her, apparently for no reason other than the pleasure of doing it. While she was in the hospital, we talked about the future."

Again, he tried to laugh.

"She actually thought I'd divorce her because she was paralyzed. Little did she know just how much I loved her."

He could not control his emotion now, and tears rolled down his cheeks.

"Forgive me. It's all so fresh, you know."

"Yes, I know. I went through it, too, when Barry was killed."

"Of course. He was murdered. Terrible, needless waste of good people. Well, I can shorten this story a good deal. I thought coming back to this place would be a good idea, to get out of the city. She said she wanted a place where she could work in peace. Somehow we hit on the idea of not telling anyone about her, and keeping our home secret. But to do that, I had to tell my father, and he agreed that if we wanted it that way, he wouldn't say anything to anyone. And he didn't. Then when he died, of course, I took over the newspaper and commercial press."

"You had to attend evening events and meetings, didn't you?"

"Yes. When I did, I stayed in town. I took a small apartment, so that people would think I wasn't married."

"And Rebecca didn't mind? I mean, it might have crossed her mind that you had something going with another woman."

"No. Not Rebecca. Nor would I ever have done such a thing. Enough unattached women thought they could seduce me, but they soon learned to back off. One night, I remember, a woman came to my apartment and pushed her way in. I don't know what she thought. Why would I fall into bed with a woman like that? Anyway, after unceremoniously kicking her out, I got dressed and drove home to my wife. She was surprised, but somehow I felt the need to be with the one I loved. It was one of the few times that I didn't get to work the next day until noon."

He lapsed into memory, and Dee waited patiently. The more he talked, the more Dee felt her own loss. Barry and she had a good life together, maybe not so devoted to each other as Marvin and Rebecca, but caring and happy. She had not cried over his death, despite that great void in her life. Now, she felt that she would cry if she didn't move on to something else.

"Was she a native of New York City?"

"No. She grew up in Altoona, Pennsylvania. She was adopted, so I know of no living relatives. Her adoptive parents are both gone."

"And you were born here in Fairchance? Went through local schools?"

"That's right. But my dad was a believer in travel as the best teacher, so we took a good many vacations in Europe, and South America. We saw most of the United States."

"What about relatives. You say Rebecca had none. Do you have relatives?"

"I do. Not here, though. My aunt Helena Reese lives in China. She's an interpreter, of all things."

Dee looked down at her notes. As far as she was concerned, Marvin had given her plenty to work with, and she felt that she should end the discussion. It must hurt him physically to talk, and emotionally to think about the past.

"I'll leave now, Marvin. You need rest, and this can't be doing you any good."

"Dee. Before you go, tell me something. Is there any possibility that you might think again about my offer to you? More than ever now, I want to unload the newspaper. I can make you a better deal."

"Oh. I...well, I have thought a bit more about it. I must say that I've grown quite fond of the city and the people I work with. I've thought that if I did purchase the paper, I'd be a working publisher. Natalie is a good editor, and Astrid is a sharp reporter and refreshingly genuine. These are all considerations that lure me toward the move. When you first made the offer, I had just given up the rehab camp, and was worn out from it. Things have changed considerably. It's gratifying to be in work as vital as the newspaper, staying current. There's a strong possibility that I might reconsider."

"That's good. Don't say any more now. When I'm out of here and up to it, we'll talk again on the matter."

"Yes. We'll do that."

TWENTY-NINE

Jason hadn't seen a woman that tall for years. Women that he had lived with all had to look up to him, and he liked that. Astrid looked like she could pick him up and throw him half way across the back yard. From what he saw of her, he'd say she was a giant pain in the ass, like most women.

Now he knew the routine at her house, when she was gone each day, and when Abram would be taking his physical therapy treatments. This was good. Monday he would get inside the house and locate that money. He was sure now that it was hidden in the cellar, probably in the base of that big fireplace chimney. The best part was that he had access to the house.

When he visited yesterday and lured Abram out for a spin in his new car—the one he rented for a week—he managed to be alone in the kitchen for a few seconds, long enough to unlock one of the windows. Now he could enter through that window, hidden from anyone's sight because of the workshop on one side and the hedge on the other side. He'd have hours to search.

Sitting in the attic window and taking note of any activity around the house, Jason was hit by a new thought. Why should he spend hours searching everywhere when it would be simple to use dynamite and blow the base of that chimney apart? It would look like parts of a crumbling old chimney had fallen down. He could do it…buy some dynamite at the hardware store, go into the house, and plant the explosive, set the fuse afire and take cover behind the stairs. How difficult could it be? Once the hiding place was opened up, he'd grab the money, and run out the back door to the line of overgrown shrubbery and trees. From there it would be easy to walk home without being noticed.

He had seen dynamite used in South Korea on road construction sites. He saw a man blast a dam once. It took more than one blast, though. The first one wasn't enough. So maybe he should use more than one stick of dynamite for the chimney. He had no one to discuss this with, but his reason told him it would take at least two sticks, maybe three.

Guilford would have taken care to have his money in a fireproof box, so an explosion wouldn't burn any of it. How many times the old man had boasted about saving his money.

"'Jason," he had said, "there's only one way to keep from losing your money. Save it in a real safe place at home. Banks are unreliable. You trust them to keep your money safe for you, but they don't. No sir. I've got mine hidden right here in my own house where I can keep watch over it."

There must be thousands of dollars stashed away, despite what Doris said. Well, yes, she said there wasn't any money, but when he got serious and threatening, he heard her say yes when he asked if it was there in the cellar. He'd never been so certain about anything, and his smart instinct always paid off. That's why when anyone wanted a job done well, they came to him. He was smart. He knew how to do everything. Almost everything, except maybe blow up something with dynamite. He didn't worry about that. Any smart man could light a fuse.

No time like the present to get prepared for Monday when Abram would go to physical therapy at two in the afternoon. Jason headed downstairs and out the door, to the rented car, drove down to Jake's Hardware, and asked for dynamite.

"I need to blow a giant rock out of my back yard," he lied. "I need five sticks."

"You know how to handle this stuff?" Jake asked.

"You think I'm an idiot? I know what to do. I've used it lotta times."

"Seems like a powerful lot just to blow up a rock. Be sure you have plenty of cover for yourself. And don't store any of the sticks that you don't use for any length of time. It's sensitive stuff, you know."

"I know. I'm no dummy."

Now dusk was settling around the backyard scene. He wondered where Doris was. Maybe Frank was having his supper. She would be inside. But wait. No. He saw her die. Didn't he? But what was she doing in that place? Sometimes he got confused about the order of things. If he thought hard, he could remember.

Okay. He had it straight now. Doris died. Astrid and Abram lived in Frank's house now. And Frank had gone someplace else.

It had become quite dark in the attic, and Jason was

ready to turn on the light, when he saw it. There it was! The black Eye, floating near that big pine tree. Of course. Now he remembered. Frank was buried there. Doris put him there.

The Eye was bigger than before.

"Go away! You haven't seen me do anything. You're just trying to make me confess to things. Well, I won't. You'll see. I won't tell what I've done. I'm okay. I'll do what I want to. Get out of my life!"

* * *

When the phone rang, Abram called to Astrid, "I'll get it."

"Ya, thanks."

In a few minutes he came into the living room where Astrid was stenciling a floral border around the top of the walls.

"Who was it?" she asked, looking down from the ladder.

"My physical therapist. He can't be there Monday. Asked me to come in Tuesday morning, instead."

"Didn't you say you were going to start doing the exercises at home?"

"I have to see the surgeon first, after four weeks. He will check my progress and I expect he'll say okay to doing the exercises here on my own. It'll be a whole lot cheaper."

"I hear that okay."

Astrid had finished two walls. She got down from the ladder and went to Abram's side.

"Well? What do you think of that?"

"Very classy. You do good work, Astrid."

The praise nearly undid her. She'd expected some smart remark from Abram. He must be showing his remorse for upsetting her. She set her paint brush into a can with water and other brushes.

"I think I want another cup of coffee. How about you?"

"No. I've had enough. You drink a lot of that stuff, don't you?"

"Ya. I do like coffee."

He sat at the table with her, with a far away look in his eyes. Astrid noticed.

"What is it, Abram? Something bothering you?"

"I was just thinking about Doris Guilford's cold-blooded murder. Still wondering if we should report the fact that the man's body is buried out there by the pine tree."

"It's been there for many years. I guess it won't hurt to wait a while. Maybe it's wrong to kill someone, but in a case like that, I can understand it."

"So can I. It doesn't make it any less murder. I'm like you in going back and forth about revealing what we know. Can't quite make up my mind."

"Well, let's just wait a bit. A few days more or less won't make any difference."

This would be the time to tell Abram about her decision to buy the farm, but Astrid wanted to be sure she could get it before telling him. As for the murder and the body buried out back, she still thought the man got what he deserved. Maybe it wasn't the Christian way of thinking, but now she believed Doris did what she had to. Frank Guilford might have killed or seriously maimed her if he wasn't stopped, just as Abram had pointed out. It was no stretch to conclude that the woman acted in self-defense. She defended herself the only way she knew that would end all her suffering.

THIRTY
MONDAY, SEPTEMBER 11, 1989

This was the big day when Astrid would see Randall King and make her offer on the farm. She got up with the sun, thinking of nothing else. A hard line had to be taken in negotiating a price. He couldn't afford to keep it, but he would balk at losing money, she was sure of that. It didn't matter. She knew what she would pay, and he could take it or leave it. Oh, she might be a bit flexible. After all, she did want the place.

Dressed and downstairs early, she started the coffee, and poured herself a glass of orange juice. When the bacon began sizzling, Abram appeared at the door.

"Mornin'. You're up early, aren't you?"

"I have a big deal this morning."

"What big deal is that?"

He dragged a chair to the table, sat down, and reached for the juice Astrid had set at his place.

She just couldn't wait to tell him about her plan, even though she felt uneasy doing it immediately. Last evening they had watched TV coverage of the accident that took Rebecca Cornell's life.

"First," she said as she dropped four eggs into the skillet, "I didn't tell you about Mrs. Cornell, did I? I mean, the part that TV didn't have."

"No. What about her?"

"The TV reporter didn't say anything about the fact that she was a composer and an artist. Dee said Mrs. Cornell didn't want anyone to know about her. They lived on that mountain top in seclusion. At least, she did. Mr. Cornell never told anyone in Fairchance about her until he asked Dee to dinner. They invited her to their home when he hoped she would agree to buy the newspaper. It was Rebecca's choice to hide like that. Everyone thought he wasn't married. Can you imagine being a recluse? Living in anonymity just seems so damned unnatural."

"Maybe. I guess if that was what she liked, we can't be a judge of it, can we?"

"No. Just seems odd. Poor woman. She was confined to a wheelchair, and chose to ignore society. I think I'd have felt like a prisoner."

"Me too. It's tough enough waiting out the healing of this bum shoulder. I get the feeling that I'm a prisoner sometimes."

Astrid saw his side glance at her and knew he was pointing out that he needed to get out of the house now and then. And, of course, that was his excuse for joining Jason Trump for a drink. It no longer mattered to her. He was free to do what he wanted to, but not to smoke or drink in her house.

"There's something else, Abram."

They sat facing each other, drinking coffee and eating Danish rolls.

"Something else. Like what?"

"Like a plan I have in mind. That's what I meant when I said I have a big deal this morning."

She finished her breakfast, and stood up to clear the table.

"A big deal doesn't tell me too much. How about another clue?"

He was in good humor this morning. Astrid thought how too bad it would be to tell him and ruin that mood. She just knew that he wouldn't be too pleased when he found out that she was planning to buy the farm from King. But why should that concern her? It was her choice. She would tell him out of courtesy, not for his approval.

Standing with her back to the sink, she folded her arms and raised her chin. Trying not to sound belligerent, she told him all at once.

"When I saw Mr. King and he asked me to write a story about the fact that he wants to sell the Chris Wolf farm he invested in, I got to thinking that maybe I would offer to buy it from him."

She saw the immediate change in Abram's expression, confirming what she had anticipated. He was not pleased to hear this. Before he could say so, she hurried on.

"I've talked with my accountant, and he's working up a tax plan for me in order to get whatever tax credit I can. I briefly told him some of my thoughts about new projects, and he approved, told me to go ahead and buy it and then go back to see him. It looks good."

She stopped talking and the room was silent. What was he thinking? Did he worry that she'd have no use for him if she bought the farm? At last, he stood up and walked into the dining room where he took his shirt from the back of her swivel chair. Pulling it on was not possible, so he just stood and waited for her to come to his aid.

Astrid unfolded her arms, relaxed her jaw, followed him, and took the shirt from him.

"So what do you think, Abram? Good plan, huh?"

Her brightness didn't move him. Was he going to talk at all? Did she care?

"Whatever you want to do, I guess."

"You don't sound pleased with the idea."

"Why should I be pleased? You won't be wanting to do all the work you had set out for me here, I take it."

"Well, no. Not exactly. But there will have to be some renovations in order to re-sell it."

"So I can do a few patch-up jobs, and then, farewell, adios, don't let the door hit your backside on your way out. That about it?"

"Well. No. If you wanted to, you could come work at the farm."

"I'm no farmer, Astrid. But I can plainly see that I'm not important, anyway. Why did you bother to tell me at all? You should have waited until you had the papers all signed and sealed, before you told me to scram."

"Abram! That's not fair. I won't tell you to scram. There will always be work to do here and at the farm."

"Beautiful. Just lovely. There will always be work. You mean a day or two a week? Or maybe an hour or two? Maybe you'll have a few stalls to muck out. Old Abram Lincoln wouldn't mind filling in for a farm hand who's out sick. Maybe an out house needs to be shoveled out, too, while he's about it."

That was it. Astrid had enough of his whining. She knew he'd take it hard, but at least he should understand her side of it. This was her future. Her decision. It wasn't as if they were married and he had a right to express opposition to something she wanted to do. He had no say in this whatsoever.

"I've got to go to work, Abram. And I'm going to see Randall King and make a purchase offer on the farm. And you can just stuff it. You have no damned say in this. What makes you think you have a right to lay a guilt trip on me just because you might not have all the work you thought you'd have from me? I've housed you and fed you, helped you while you could do nothing. Now that's the thanks I get. So just sulk all you want to. I'll see you later."

"Boy, you're somethin', ain't ya? Can't you find more to throw in my face? Maybe some rotten eggs or tomatoes? The real mistake that I made was to let you talk me into taking your charity."

"Oh!" She was exasperated. "Abram. you're...you're impossible."

His voice rose to the level of hers.

"Maybe. But I'm no beggar, and I won't be beholding to you."

"Fine. That's just fine by me. And I'm not your wife. I don't need your permission or your approval for my actions. You're an adult and you can damned well take care of yourself. And I can plan my life by myself without your help."

"Well, we both agree on all that. Have a good day."

She slammed the door behind her and got into the Jeep, spinning the tires in her haste to get away from Abram. There were days when that man made her so mad she could just strangle him. How could Doris Guilford wait so long to do in that brute she was married to? More power to her for killing the bastard. Astrid understood the urge precisely. Men!

"Well, the sun doesn't rise and set for you, Mr. Abram Lincoln. Stay out of my life and we'll get along just fine."

THIRTY-ONE

Arriving at the office, Astrid found only Dee at her desk, looking as if she hadn't slept in a couple of nights.

"Natalie is across the hall picking up the crash site pictures," Dee said. "How are you this morning, Astrid?"

"Just fine."

She sat down so hard her chair rolled back and hit the wall.

"You seem upset. Something troubling you?"

"Nothing a damned double-barrel shotgun wouldn't take care of."

"Astrid! I've never seen you like this. What in the world's wrong?"

"I'll be okay. Just a bit of a row with Abram this morning. It'll pass."

"I'm a good listener, if you want to talk about it."

"I know. But I don't think so. I won't be here too long this morning. I've got to get this work cleaned up."

Natalie came through the door holding several large prints and studying them as she walked to her desk.

"Mornin' Astrid."

"Natalie."

"You're going to see Mr. King this morning?"

"Yes. I certainly am. No damned man is going to stand in the way of my making that farm my place."

Natalie barely heard what she said, but Dee did.

"Abram doesn't want you to do it?" she asked.

"No, he doesn't. He got his back up this morning and acted like I was deliberately taking work away from him."

"Oh."

Dee obviously knew when to keep quiet, and Astrid appreciated that. She didn't need anyone advising her to make up and work it out. With some people, there was no working it out. She'd go ice skating in hell before she'd say she was sorry to Abram. Not only had she let him camp out in her house, but she'd contacted her lawyer to take care of his bills. She didn't throw that in his face, but she should have. She should have said, 'Maybe you can pay me back what I paid for your brother's medical bills.' She should have said, 'Maybe you'd prefer to go to a nursing home while you're recuperating, and pay for that bill yourself.' She should have said, 'You can pay me for the food you've eaten while you were under my roof.' She could have said a lot more than she did. The day wasn't over. They'd probably have another round when she got home, but she wouldn't think about that now. There was work to do.

* * *

By late morning, Astrid was sitting in Randall King's office, where he waited in his big chair to hear if she was going to write a good article about his decision to sell the farm. Instead, she gave him the bad news first.

"Natalie says we won't be publishing a story about the sale of your farm," she said.

His neck began to turn pink beneath the white collar, slowly climbing over the first layer of his double chin. He remained quiet, like a cat watching the bird he'll have for lunch. But Astrid wasn't about to be Mr. King's lunch today.

"Instead," she said, "I'm here to assure that you do sell the farm, and today, if you agree."

Now he sat up straight and leaned forward with his arms on the desk.

"Today? What are you talking about?"

"I want to buy that property from you, Mr. King. And I'm here to make a reasonable offer this morning."

"You? What do you want with a farm?"

"I was raised on a farm. I know how to manage one, and I want to get back to the land where I'll be my own boss."

"Hard to believe a woman wants to take on that kind of operation," he said.

"Well this woman does. And you should be grateful for that."

If she sounded a tad aggressive, it was because she still burned over Abram's reaction, and she didn't care to hear any more negative talk about buying a farm. And she certainly was in no mood to be accused of being a woman and, therefore, unable to do the work of a man.

King took a cigar from the center desk drawer, snipped off the end, and lit it, noisily sucking on it seven or eight times before it glowed.

"I'm asking five hundred thousand for it, you know," he said, holding the cigar like a lady holds a cup of tea, his pinky bent outward.

"I know," she said. She had no intention of allowing him to make a profit off her. "But I'm not offering that. My offer is three hundred thousand."

"Ha! You think I'll take a loss on this investment? No way."

"Then I guess we have no more to talk about, Mr. King. Good luck selling your farm."

Astrid got up and started for the door. Would he stop her? Or would he just let her walk away? This was the tricky part about negotiating, especially when she wanted that property so badly.

When he spoke, she squeezed her eyes shut. Yes!

"Wait a minute, Miss Thorpe. Don't be too hasty, now. We should be able to compromise. After all, the property is worth a whole lot more than five hundred thousand, but I can understand. You're probably worried that you won't be able to get a mortgage."

She turned back to face him. Keeping a perfectly blank expression was difficult, but she managed.

"Who said anything about a mortgage? What makes you think I'd need to get one to buy that farm?"

King withdrew the soggy end of the cigar from his mouth and put it on the amber glass ashtray where other brown cigar gobs had rested for days. Her words hit a vulnerable target. This was still more that he had not anticipated.

"You mean…? Well, of course you need a mortgage.

Anyone earning what you earn as a reporter can't possibly have enough money to pay in cash."

"Oh, Mr. King, I'm sure you've heard of the Axelgren Farms brand name. Its products are sold throughout the state of Maine, and have been for fifty years."

"And what does that have to do with you?"

"Everything. Axel Thorpe was my grandfather. He came to the U.S. at the age of twenty and created Axelgren Farms. I inherited a fortune from him. So, you see, I can afford to buy that farm. But I assure you, I don't need it. I can walk away and just forget it. The only real reason I want to buy it is to keep it as a productive farm property, not divided into housing lots or sold for a shopping mall. You have my offer. Take it or leave it."

He eyed her with an I-don't-believe-it scowl, but he was thinking. Astrid liked that.

"I won't take less than four twenty-five for it."

"Oh? If you keep the farm, you will have to oversee a lot of upkeep in order to expect a sale for farming purposes. You'll have taxes and insurances to pay. You'll need to keep the fields mowed so they won't all go back to woodland. The buildings will soon need paint. Roofs will need new shingles. Each year you hold title to it, you lose money, big money. Your best bet now is to let it go at my price and cut your losses. You were hasty in buying it, if not downright unethical."

"How about four hundred?"

Astrid shook her head.

"No. I, too, will need to put a lot of money into the

operation. I will compromise and pay what you paid. Three hundred fifty thousand. Not a penny more."

He stood up, pushed his chair back, and leaned across the desk with his hand extended.

"You've got a deal, Miss Thorpe. Can't say I'm pleased with it, but I need to unload that burden, so it's yours for three hundred fifty thousand."

She was sure he thought he'd pulled the wool over her eyes, but in fact, she was prepared to go to four hundred thousand.

"I'll contact my attorney and have him draw up the papers," he said. "Then I'll let you know when and where to meet us. Probably won't take more than two weeks. In the meantime, he'll want a check as surety. I don't know. Say ten thousand?"

"Say five thousand. You know where I live and where I work. And I know the same about you."

"You are a hard woman to do business with," King said.

But all the while he had a smile on his face that Astrid had not seen there before.

THIRTY-TWO

Even if it hadn't been Monday, Astrid wouldn't have gone home and risk getting into another argument with Abram. Anyway, Monday was too busy a day to take more time off after her negotiation with King. She stopped at the supermarket, bought three subs and a bag of potato chips, and went back to the office, where Dee and Natalie were still working at eleven-thirtry.

"Hi, you two," she said. "I got subs for the three of us. Hope you like turkey. I'll go make the coffee now."

"Thanks, Astrid." Natalie said. "I was just beginning to think about lunch. There's cheese and bread in the refrigerator. I planned to have a cheese sandwich. I like the idea of a sub much better."

"Everything go okay with King?" Dee asked. "Did you make a deal on the farm?"

"Ya. Sure did. I'm buying it for just what he paid. I wanted to pay less, but would have gone to four hundred thousand, if I had to. He was asking five hundred thousand. He thought he could still make a bundle on it."

"Good for you."

"Anything new on Mr. Cornell?" Astrid said.

"He's about the same," Dee said. "I talked with him after you left, and he sounded very depressed. Between the loss of Rebecca and all the painkillers he's taking, I suppose that's to be expected."

"After lunch, Astrid," Natalie said, "I want you to call the two funeral homes and find out which one is handling Mrs. Cornell's funeral. If they have any details now, take them. If not, ask when they will have them. Also find out who's handling the funeral details. Dee didn't talk with Mr. Cornell long enough to find out. Not her fault. The nurse had to do her work."

Astrid nodded and went to the lounge to prepare things for lunch. If there was anything she hated to do, it was talk with morticians. What a rotten job they had. One thing about it though, they never ran out of work.

* * *

Jason watched the time carefully, while studying Astrid's house. No one seemed to be around today. Neighbors around here weren't exactly chummy, he thought, not like the family and neighbors he had in South Korea. He was surrounded by people most of the time. This was a whole lot better. He liked being alone. He liked plotting a crime, too. The operation of the break-in and the way to proceed after that were a creation of his imagination. He had the mind and skill for it, and he had the will, something most people just didn't have. Caution was the key ingredient to being an intelligent thief or executioner. Rule out all possibility of failure by thinking it all through, mapping the terrain, knowing when the time was right to strike.

Against all odds, he could always tell when he could get cash or jewels or other valuables. If there had ever been a doubt that Guilford had stashed away money, Jason had erased it. There couldn't be any doubt about it. His instinct told him that a man like that, greedy and miserly, never took chances, and he probably wasn't too open with his wife about the money. Maybe she knew that he had hidden it in the cellar, but he doubted that he told her how to get at it. He just wouldn't. His recollection of the man and what he said one day when Jason was fifteen was burned into his memory.

"Jason," he said, "you're very young yet. But let me tell you something, and don't ever forget it. When you get married, never tell your wife how much money you make or how much you've saved. You put that money somewhere that she won't find it, somewhere like a secret place built into a chimney, and you say nothing to her. She'll hound you for money, but you dole out only what she needs for household expenses. Otherwise, she'll spend all that you make. If she knows where to find the money, she'll take it and spend it on luxuries, things she doesn't need. You understand me, son?"

Jason understood then, and he understood now after his own married life. The reference to a chimney hiding place was significant. Frank was hiding wads of cash in the base of the fireplace, and he kept it from Doris. Maybe she knew that it was somewhere down there, but not just where. She wouldn't have been searching the base of the fireplace anyway, not a foolish woman like her.

It was now two o'clock. Abram would have gone to his physical therapy session by now. It was time to go get himself a small fortune, at least enough to carry him through a few months, maybe even keep this terrific car.

"Now it's time to do some blasting for gold, my good man. Mr. Guilford, thank you for your miserly ways, and thank you for tipping me off. You were a man after my own heart. Maybe I should say before my own heart."

He didn't often laugh out loud, but he did now. This was too good an opportunity not to be happy about it. Only he knew the secrets of that house, and only he would cash in on them.

* * *

Lunch over, Astrid did the calling that Natalie requested and learned that the funeral arrangements had not yet been made. The funeral director was to go to the hospital and work with Mr. Cornell on the wording of the obituary, but would not have a service until he was able to attend it.

Two women and one man walked in with notices they wanted in this week's publication. A quick check with the police station revealed that there had been an incident of domestic battery, resulting in the man's going to the emergency room for stitches after his wife cut him on the arm with a paring knife. Otherwise, there had been no significant activity to report.

At two o'clock, Astrid's phone buzzed and she was told that her brother was on the line for her.

"Gunnar," she said. "What's the matter?"

"Nothing's the matter. Why do you always say that when I call?"

"Because something usually is wrong when you call."

"Well it's not this time. I've done it."

"What have you done?"

"I convinced Mr. Carney of Construcorp to come take a look at my farm. He liked the sound of it, and even agreed with me that people will go to a mall no matter where's it's located."

Astrid couldn't speak. She was going into farming and her brother was leaving the farm life. Somehow it all seemed too weird. She could have gone home and kept the family business, but thought Gunnar would come around and finally keep it up himself. Besides, she knew he would ask a whole lot more for the properties than they were worth. He was so anxious to be a very rich man that he just might price himself out of the picture with Mr. Carney.

"Astrid? Aren't you going to say something? You don't approve."

"It's not that, Gunnar. If you can do it, fine. I was just thinking how too bad it is to end the family business."

"Sure. You could buy it, you know. But you don't care enough about it to come through. We could trade the money Grampa left to you for the farm he left to me."

"That's unfair, and you know it. He left you money enough to carry on. I've made my life here in Fairchance, and I think I'll always live here now."

"Ya. I know. You always did get the best of everything. No hard labor for you. I guess that's the way it should be. But now if I make this deal, I'll be able to do something else, something I want to do, too."

"What is that?"

"I don't know just yet. But I'll find something less

tedious than this grunt work all the time. Keeping my nose to the grindstone day after day, and being a slave to planting seasons, and to cows and milking hours, isn't my idea of pleasure. I guess if you had to do it, you'd understand."

"I always liked the work."

"Ya, you liked it as long as you could leave it when you wanted to. You were never tied down to it, like I was."

There was no point in talking with Gunnar about it. His mind was set on selling out, and she did understand, even though she didn't approve. She wouldn't tell him that she was making her own commitment to the life he wanted to give up. He would only repeat that she should buy him out. It wasn't the farm work she didn't like. It was more what she did like…being in the city of Fairchance. And, if she bought King's farm, she could still write part time for the newspaper. That, in her view, was indeed the best of two worlds.

"I guess you're right, Gunnar. If Construcorp agrees to buy the place, then I say God bless you in the deal. Just be careful not to beat yourself by pricing it all too high."

"There you go. What would I do without your advice? As if I couldn't figure that one out myself."

"Dammit, I didn't mean that you couldn't work it all out. I was just thinking out loud, that's all. I know you'll do everything you can to sell, so I wish you luck."

"Good. Now I feel so much better."

Why, she wondered, are men like that? Why do they have that put-upon reaction to everything a woman says?

"Gunnar, don't be angry with me. You're my brother. You don't need my advice, and I know it."

There, she groveled. Maybe he could speak in a civil tone now.

"Ya. I know," he said. "Sorry about calling you at the office. I just couldn't wait to tell someone the news. I talked with the two top board members today, and they really do sound interested."

"When are they going to go see the place?"

"Next Monday, they said."

"Sounds good. Thanks for calling me. And I really do wish you luck and hope you get what you want out of it."

"Thanks, Astrid."

She hung up with a feeling of great loss, knowing that the name Axelgren would soon become extinct. Grampa would be sick over it if he had lived to see the day that his grandson had so little regard for the family business and the family name.

THIRTY-THREE

Jason squeezed through the window and into Astrid's kitchen with no difficulty. He had learned a long time ago not to take it for granted that he was alone in a house, even when he knew everyone's scheduled absences, so he stood quietly for a few minutes and listened to each tick of the clock and each gust of wind hitting a loose shutter. The weather wasn't the best for this kind of operation. Too much outside noise, but he determined that no one was here and proceeded down the cellar stairs.

As old rock wall cellars with dirt floors went, this one was clean, dry, and deep enough so that he didn't have to crouch to walk. Of course, being only a little over five seven made it easy to get around in smaller spaces. The taller men and women like Abram and Astrid must have a real hard time in a place like this, where his own head just missed hitting overhead beams.

He went directly to the bottom of the fireplace chimney and found that it was set on a wide concrete base. Would the money be in that base or in the bricks themselves, he wondered. He hoped he had brought enough dynamite. Looked to him like it would take a lot to open a hole in each side and on the front, and that was the only way he could locate the hiding nook where the money was stashed. His guess was that there was a good-sized hollow, and a way to open the front of that hole, but he didn't have time to hunt for it. Why should he when he could just blow it open?

There was loose mortar here and there, and he used his fingernail to dig bits out, allowing room for him to insert the sticks. The fuses were quite long. He should have no trouble lighting the three of them and getting back to the stairway where he'd have protection beneath the top platform.

He had just finished digging out the last mortar for a stick of dynamite when a noise startled him. It sounded like a door closing upstairs. Maybe he wasn't alone. He stood perfectly still and waited and listened, but he heard no more.

"Must be the wind," he mumbled, and turned back to the job at hand. With the three sticks implanted as solidly as he could get them, he tucked the other two sticks in a back pocket. From a front pocket, he took a lighter, flicked it open, and turned the wheel for flame. Quickly, he lit one after another of the wicks, and dashed behind the protective stairs. Squatting down, he looked around the stairs to be sure that the wicks were burning. In the light from their flames, he now saw what he hadn't noticed before. Beside the chimney were two large bags of fertilizer. He recalled something about fertilizer.

"Nitrogen."

He felt his neck hairs move. It was too late. The dynamite was ready to blast. He looked around for better protection, but he had no place to go. The fertilizer might not explode, so no worry, he told himself.

Then he saw it. The Eye, black and staring, floated over the fertilizer bags.

"No! No! You won't win. I'll kill you, Eye. You've dogged me long enough."

Growling like a mad dog, Jason ran toward the Eye, seeing nothing else, thinking only that he could tear that Eye apart with his own hands. It was growing larger and larger. The eye-Eye- EYE, enlarging, pulling until the two merged and blew into oblivion.

* * *

The day was winding down by three o'clock, with almost everything ready for the week's publication, and Astrid now started to think about a couple of interviews she would be making for next week's issue of *The Bugle*. She began to write down questions.

But she couldn't concentrate. She stared at the wall while her thoughts turned to her relationship with Abram. Maybe she wasn't being sympathetic enough about him. After all, living together for a couple of weeks, they had shared private thoughts, read Mrs. Guilford's diary together, laughed over silly little things. He had definitely shown interest in her. If she were honest with herself, she had more than a little interest in him. Perhaps she had been too demanding, too ready to discard their friendship.

Why did she become so upset when he didn't congratulate her about the decision to purchase the farm? In her heart she had known that he'd be disturbed by it, and she knew why. Yet, when it happened, she acted like he was of no importance to her. And that wasn't true. He was more important to her than she ever dreamed any man would be.

She felt a strange combination of emotions. All that self-congratulatory pride now began to turn to self-loathing for hurting Abram. She now wished she had addressed his concern over his future before she went ahead with making the offer on the farm. Maybe she wouldn't have done it after all. Maybe she should have thought about his welfare and realized that the way things were, she could give him plenty of work, a home while he was doing it, and possibly more chance for them to become better acquainted. Maybe if that had happened, he would have come to the conclusion that they were good together and should remain so for the rest of their lives.

The way things stood now, they might never get to that place, and it saddened her to think of what might have developed had she not been so gung-ho to pursue an agricultural career, be the boss, and run something big and worthwhile. Hells bells, she thought, the newspaper was about as worthwhile as anything could be. Why was she so damned stupid?

She lowered her eyes to the notepad in front of her and pretended to be writing, all the while close to tears over the knowledge that Abram and she would never have the same relationship again. It had been such a good feeling to go home and know that he would be there to discuss the day's work or plans for the renovations. Even reading the diary had been a shared experience that created hot discussion on the pros and cons of the murder, and Mrs. Guilford's long-suffering years with that devil.

A loud boom rattled the office windows and shook Astrid from her introspection.

"What the hell was that?" she said.

"Probably blasting at that road repair site. We love those summertime road construction projects," Natalie said. "We'll wait a few minutes before making a call. No one will know anything yet."

"We should have a police monitor," Dee said.

"We did, but it broke down and hasn't been replaced or repaired. When you become publisher, you can authorize the purchase of a new one," Natalie said.

"Getting the Christmas wish list in a little early, aren't you?"

"You bet. While you're signing vouchers, you can do one for a new coffee pot, too. That old thing is ready for the dump."

"Seems like we could all share the expense of a new coffee maker," Dee said.

"No, no. That's for the office. I buy only for my home, not for the business. I put enough of my time in here."

Dee shook her head.

"I hear mutiny already?" she said. "Maybe I'd better not take over. I didn't know there would be all this sudden dissension."

"Oh, we're just beginning to make demands. Wait until you're the top dog. We'll come up with a list that'll knock your socks off."

"Did I miss something?" Astrid asked. "Are you really going to buy it, Dee?"

"I think so. We haven't agreed on anything yet. But Mr. Cornell did speak of it again when I was at the hospital, and I told him I would give it serious thought. I told Natalie while you were gone this morning."

"Well, that's great news. Damned good news," Astrid said.

She remembered how she felt when she first came to interview for the job. Her clothes had not been an issue, as she had expected them to be with two fashion plates next to her. Nor had they said anything about her rough speech. Of course, she had been working on that, and hardly ever said off-color things here at the office now.

Natalie answered the phone on the first buzz. Her face sobered, signaling a problem.

"Where?" she asked. A pause, then, "Oh, no."

Her eyes widened and she focused on Astrid.

"Okay. Thanks. I'll tell her."

She hung up and left her hand on the phone. Her mouth twisted as she thought how to tell the others.

"That was Police Chief Nolan. The explosion was at a house."

Natalie kept her eyes on Astrid.

"I don't know how to say this except to say it, Astrid. It's your house, I'm afraid."

"*My* house. What happened?"

"They don't know. They're fighting the fire now and trying to keep the flames from spreading around the place. Dee, I want you to take a camera and to follow Astrid there."

"My God. Abram! What happened to him? Did the chief say anything about Abram?"

"He said…oh, dear. I'm so sorry. Chief Nolan said they think there are…that is, there may be a body in the basement, but they can't get at it yet."

Astrid felt dizzy and nauseous all at once. Abram's body.

"What could he have been doing?"

"Maybe you should take Astrid with you, Dee," Natalie said. "I don't think she should drive."

Astrid felt like she was stepping too high as they walked out to the car, but she couldn't seem to control her feet. She said no more. She couldn't. Without Abram life wouldn't be worth living. He couldn't be dead. She needed to make up with him. She couldn't have it end like this.

When they turned onto Main Street, Astrid saw smoke billowing over the city. Everything must be all gone, she thought. What could have happened? She didn't dare think of Abram. All she could do was pray that he got out safely. If he didn't make it, she hoped death was instantaneous.

A police car blocked the entrance to the cul-de-sac when they got there. Dee parked her SUV on the side of the adjoining street, and Astrid slid out quickly to run to Lilac Lane. It looked like the aftermath of a giant woodland fire with so much smoke. She knew her house was gone, but what about Abram?

Where did all the people come from? Lilac Lane sidewalks were lined with men, women, and children. Police were trying to keep them from hindering the work of the fire fighters. Astrid didn't know she had so many neighbors. She darted in and out of the crowd, all the while studying faces to see if Abram was one of them, but he wasn't. When she got as close as she could to her burning house, she ran beside a fire fighter while he was pulling a hose toward the ruins.

"Did a man get out of the house alive?" she asked.

"No one came out," he said.

She stopped running and went to the closest lawn, where she fell to her knees. Of course no one came out. If a body was found, it had to be Abram's.

"Abram. Abram," she chanted.

Dee was now at Astrid's side and knelt down to hold her.

"Maybe he wasn't home," she said.

"Yes, he was. He didn't go to therapy today. He was alone in there. What happened? Why? Oh God. Why?"

At last, she stopped sobbing, and turned from her knees to a sitting position, holding her head. She had no strength to get to her feet, but sat choking on smoke sweeping down on gusts of wind. Her mind was blank except for the one thought: *Abram was killed in my house.*

Someone shook her shoulder. She looked up and saw that it was a police officer.

"Ma'am, you should move away. There could be another explosion. Here, let me help you up."

Barely aware of what was happening, she let herself be pulled up and aided to a less smoky area down the street. Truck engines droned and voices yelled, people ran all about her, lights flashed, and her lungs felt like they would burst. But still Astrid saw and heard very little. Stunned and devastated by the double loss in such a manner, she couldn't think. She watched as the fire fighters brought flames under control.

"How could it have happened?" she asked of no one in particular.

As her thoughts began to meld again, she became even more devastated by the memory of her parting with Abram. They were both angry. How could she have left him like that? Why didn't she wait to leave after they had made up? She could still have said that she would re-think her plan, and she should have told him that he was more important to her than owning a farm.

"Oh Abram," she moaned. "I'm so sorry."

Dee, who had gone to take more photos, now returned. She put her arm around Astrid's waist.

"Come on. We have all we need here. I'll take you to my place and you can stay with me."

"I have to make funeral arrangements for Abram, and buy a cemetery lot for him. And for me. We'll be buried side by side."

"Astrid. Don't think about it yet. You can face that tomorrow. For now, you'll go and lie down. If you need something to help you sleep, I'll get my doctor to prescribe something."

"Ya. Prescribe. I…my home is gone. Abram's gone. I…I don't…I need to make funeral arrangements."

"I know. Come on. Let's get to the car."

Only minutes later, Dee parked her vehicle next to her bungalow.

"This is it. Let's go inside and get you settled."

"What's this?" Astrid said. "Where are we?"

"At my house. You need to calm yourself. Lie down and sleep a while."

"No. There's work to be done. I want to go back to the office with you. I can't rest. Let's get going."

"But you are in no condition to work."

"Ya. I am. It's what I have to do."

"Well, okay. If it's too much, you can rest in the lounge."

Dee backed the SUV out and drove toward the office, while Astrid muttered over and over, "I need to make funeral arrangements."

THIRTY-FOUR
TUESDAY, SEPTEMBER 12, 1989

She thought she would never be able to sleep again, but when Astrid got into the bed Dee had made up for her, she dropped off quickly. She woke up when she felt a light touch. Dee was standing by the bed.

"What?" she asked. "Where am I?"

"You're in my house, Astrid. You've slept for fourteen hours. It's two o'clock, time to wake up."

"Fourteen hours? I never slept that long in my life."

Then it all came flooding in.

"Abram. My house. Oh, God. How can I go on?"

"I know. I've been through it myself. You think you can't bear up under that load of sorrow, but you will. The sharp edge will dull down after a while, and you'll be able to live your life again. For now, just take each day and try not to go too deeply into the sorrow pit."

Astrid swung her legs out of the bed and sat there looking down at her bare feet. She felt awkward in a nightgown that Dee let her use. It barely reached her knees.

"Why did it explode? Was he doing something, I wonder. I need to get my car and go see the place. Oh, this is publication day. I need to get to the office now."

"No, you don't. The paper has gone to bed. Everything's

done. Just take a shower and get dressed. I'll have breakfast ready for you when you come down."

"I'll have to wear yesterday's clothes. I'll get some new things today, and I'll have to go to the bank and get all that reorganized. All my papers and records were in the house. Oh, what a mess."

"Did you insure here in Fairchance, through one of our agents?"

"Ya. I'll go there, too. Dee, do you know if they've taken Abram's body out of the rubble yet?"

"I asked that question. They've taken him to Ownbey's Funeral Home."

"Let's see. That's on...?"

"It's on Winter Street."

"Ya. Okay."

The painful day started, the day when sunlight turned murky, when every movement required concentration, and Astrid felt drained of lifeblood.

* * *

Not wanting to wear any of Dee's doll clothes again, the first stop she made was at the bank in order to withdraw cash, thankful that she carried her check and bank books in her handbag. Next, she bought clothes at Milady's-- jeans, shirts, PJs and underwear. At the urging of the shop owner, Estelle, Astrid chose a black pants suit and white satin blouse for the funeral.

Arriving at Lilac Lane afterward, she saw that the curious were still parading by the wreckage of her home. One man was poking around the ruins with a long prod.

She hurried from her Jeep to the man. The nerve. Looking for something to salvage.

"Hey, you. What the hell do you think you're doing? This is still private property."

He turned around to face her. To make matters worse, he wore a white cup-like mask over his nose and mouth. She looked left and right to see if there might be a police officer close by. She'd have the thief arrested.

He pulled the mask down under his chin, like a doctor coming out of surgery.

"Are you the owner?" he asked.

"Ya, I'm the owner. And I'll have you arrested for trespassing."

"Hold your water, lady. I'm the insurance inspector. Name's Nelson Colby. I have some questions to ask you."

"You got here quick."

"I'm just thirty minutes away, in the Bangor office. How long have you lived here, Miss Thorpe?"

"Not quite a month."

She looked down at the still smoking, unidentifiable charred mounds in the cellar. There was nothing to salvage. She felt a wave of nausea realizing that one of those burned clumps had been Abram.

"Do you know what exploded?" she asked.

"Not yet. But we will."

His tone was accusatory, and she eyed him closely. For a man who raked around in ash, he was remarkably clean, his short hair was evenly trimmed. He wore a dark gray silky suit with a white shirt and light blue tie. Even at a distance she could smell his strong after shave. To Astrid, the man looked prissy.

"Good," she said.

"I expect you have an inventory of items that were lost."

"I lost a friend. At the moment he's the only *inventory* I can think of."

Her anger was rising. It was too soon to be confronted with something like inventory. Too soon for anything except to bury her dear Abram.

"Well, you'll need to make out an inventory as soon as you can, and list the value of each item. Let's see," he flipped several sheets on his clipboard, "you have the place insured for twenty thousand more than the purchase price."

"Ya. We were making renovations. The market value of the property would have risen when they were finished."

"I see."

He flipped through more sheets and stopped to write notes. He then looked from the burned remains to the large open lot and back to Astrid.

"Very farsighted of you," he said. "Sometimes building from scratch is easier than renovating, isn't it?"

His implication was too obvious; his smirk, obnoxious.

"I'll ignore your sarcasm, Mr. Colby, because I know my emotions are raw. But let me tell you this. I lost the dearest friend I've ever had, and the best man I've ever known in this fire. I have no patience for your mincing around here, the day after my loss, making a covert accusation. You can pay insurance on the house or not. I don't give a damn one way or the other. But I will give you a free bit of advice. Go get some training in human relations. And leave off the after shave. You stink."

Hands fisted at her sides, she strode off to her Jeep and drove away, leaving an open-mouthed insurance inspector, as well as a cluster of onlookers, watching her departure.

* * *

Before returning to Dee's house, Astrid stopped at the office to pick up a paper. Everyone had gone home for the remainder of the day. Certain that the story about her fire would be difficult for her to read, she sat at her desk to read it in private. There on page one, was the headline, *Mystery Explosion Takes Life,* over Dee's story and photos. When she read about Abram's body being found, the pain stabbed her so hard that she bent her head and cried.

"Why? I wish it had been me instead of you, Abram. I shouldn't have had you there. You'd have been spared then. I should have just advanced you money to take care of yourself until you could work. Why didn't I do that?"

Again she thought of their last time together, and her sobs became even louder. She was so angry with him. He died with that last impression of her. If only she could take it all back and tell him she was sorry. If only.

She felt like her heart couldn't take the pain of it all. How could life be so cruel? He was young, strong, full of energy. Why was life taken from him? Why was he taken from her? And what caused that explosion? It couldn't have been Abram's doing. There were no explosives in the house. It had to have been the work of someone who hated her.

Randall King? He hated her. But why would he destroy her home, maybe even her if she had been there? He stood to get his investment back through her. No, that didn't figure.

Her mind began racing over the past few months and even farther back to find someone who might wish to do her harm. All she came up with, beyond King, was the high school basketball coach, and she didn't believe that he really hated her. They had talked amicably when she picked up the basketball schedule Thursday. So who?

"If someone did this, then it's murder. It would mean that Abram was murdered. I'll have to talk with the sheriff. He'll know what to do."

She had left the office yesterday without clearing off her desk, so she began to do that now. The telephone startled her, and she debated whether to answer it. The office was officialy closed. However, since she was alone, she answered.

"*Bugle* office. Astrid Thorpe."

"Astrid. Where have you been? I've been trying and trying to reach you."

She nearly dropped the phone. Breathe, she told herself.

"Abram? How...I thought you were dead."

"Dead! Why would you think that?"

"Where are you?"

"I'm in Bath. I left you a note. Didn't you see it? Why did you think I was dead?"

"My God, Abram. I can't believe it. Oh my God."

"Astrid. You all right?"

"No. Yes. I am now."

She trembled so hard, she had to use both hands to hold the phone.

"But who died, then? Oh I'm so glad to hear your voice. You're in Bath? How did you get there? Why are you there? What have you been doing?"

"Dave Waters...you know, the man who helps me on odd jobs...came by after you left for work. He was going to the shipyard to see if he could get a permanent job and thought I might like the ride. Since I couldn't write, I had him write you a note. Didn't you get it? What's going on?"

"No, I didn't go home at noon. Haven't you seen the news or read a paper? My house exploded, and a body was found in the rubble. I thought it was you."

"Your house exploded! How did that happen? I haven't seen a TV or newspaper since I left Fairchance yesterday. Whose body is it then?"

"That's what I'd like to know, especially since you are officially dead, according to all the reports."

"I can't believe this. How bad is it damaged?"

"It's all gone. Nothing left. But at least you're alive. Oh my God. I thought I'd lost you forever."

"If only you had seen the note."

"The explosion happened in the afternoon."

They both fell silent, then Abram laughed.

"Well, I guess I'm right up there with Mark Twain. Reports of my death are greatly exaggerated."

Astrid laughed, too, all the while trying to wipe away the tears with one hand. She found it difficult to do when new tears flowed against her will.

"I just called to tell you that I'm coming back tonight. I missed physical therapy today. I guess I can't crawl back to you to beg for a place to stay, then."

"Yes you can. I'll take a couple of rooms at the motel. Please come back to me."

"Where will I see you when I get there?"

"When are you coming?"

"I should be there in three hours."

Astrid looked at the clock.

"Meet me here at the office. Your friend driving you back?"

"Yeah. He got the job and will be moving down here. I'll have him drop me off at your office, then."

"Abram. I am so sorry for all I said to you. I was wrong. You're more important than a farm to me. Please understand."

"Hey. Let's just forget it. I'm sorry, too. You were right. If you want to make a change, it's your right to do it. Cheer up, if you can after losing your house. We'll sort this all out when I get there tonight. And don't forget. You owe me a dinner."

"Abram! I do not."

Her heart beat faster when he roared with laughter. Was there anything so good in the world as to hear the voice of someone you thought had died? Especially if it was someone you loved.

Astrid stared at the phone for a long time after she hung up, thinking about the miracle that just happened. If she lived to be a hundred, nothing could possibly surpass this.